"You Really Are A Cool One, Aren't You?"

Patrick commented. "And a good little actress, too. You spend weeks running from me—or pretending to. And now that I'm here, you hardly bat an eye." A newborn suspicion leapt into Patrick's mind. Had he been too blinded by his distraction to see a tactic meant to make him react exactly as he had?

He began to circle Jordana, speaking as he went. "You aren't what I'm accustomed to. You didn't react as I expected. I love a challenge, a dare. You were both."

"You think I deliberately set out to be a dare?" Jordana asked.

"Something like that." He was still moving, his eyes on her, taking in the lines of her body, feeling his body tighten in response. If his accusations were true, then, dammit, she did it well. All of it. The dare, the enticement. The desire. He wanted her even if she was a schemer....

Dear Reader,

Annette Broadrick fans (and you know who you all are!) rejoice. Annette's *Man of the Month, Where There Is Love,* is here! This is the story you've all been waiting for: superspy Max Moran *finally* meets his match! I'm not going to tell you a single thing about this fantastic book; you've just got to read it for yourselves.

May is also chock-full of books by authors I know you love. Let's start with BJ James's *Tears of the Rose,* written in BJ's uniquely unforgettable style. Next, Leslie Davis Guccione returns with *Rough and Ready,* a title that describes her hero perfectly!

Expect the unexpected in Joan Johnston's *A Little Time in Texas,* and thrill to Justine Davis's dramatic *Upon the Storm.* And last, but not least, is *Talk of the Town* by Beverly Barton, in which it's not just the weather that gets steamy in Riverton, Mississippi.

As for next month . . . well, you're all in for an exciting treat. Believe it or not, it's the ten-year anniversary of Silhouette Desire, which was launched back in June 1982. To celebrate, I've convinced six of your favorite Desire authors to participate in a very special program, JUNE GROOMS, in which six sinfully sexy heroes are saying goodbye to the single life—forever. Don't miss it!

All the best,

Lucia Macro
Senior Editor

BJ JAMES

TEARS OF THE ROSE

SILHOUETTE *Desire*®

Published by Silhouette Books New York

America's Publisher of Contemporary Romance

SILHOUETTE BOOKS
300 East 42nd St., New York, N.Y. 10017

TEARS OF THE ROSE

ISBN: 0-373-05709-1

First Silhouette Books printing May 1992

All the characters in this book have no existence outside the imagination of the author and have no relation whatsoever to anyone bearing the same name or names. They are not even distantly inspired by any individual known or unknown to the author, and all incidents are pure invention.

® and ™: Trademarks used with authorization. Trademarks indicated with ® are registered in the United States Patent and Trademark Office, the Canada Trade Mark Office and in other countries.

Printed in the U.S.A.

Books by BJ James

Silhouette Desire

The Sound of Goodbye #332
Twice in a Lifetime #396
Shiloh's Promise #529
Winter Morning #595
Slade's Woman #672
A Step Away #692
Tears of the Rose #709

BJ JAMES

married her high school sweetheart straight out of college and soon found that books were delightful companions during her lonely nights as a doctor's wife. But she never dreamed she'd be more than a reader, never expected to be one of the blessed, letting her imagination soar, weaving magic of her own.

BJ has twice been honored by the Georgia Romance Writers with their prestigious Maggie Award for Best Short Contemporary Romance. She has also received the *Romantic Times* Critic's Choice Award.

One

———

"**T**hen we are in agreement, Mr. Briggs." It was not a question. None of the three men at the table pretended it was. Patrick McCallum leaned back in his chair, silent now. Waiting. One finger tapped idly on the stem of a crystal goblet, and a pleasant smile hovered on his lips. He appeared relaxed, completely focused.

Hundreds of feet below, traffic moved at a frantic pace. Sounds of the street clashed with the sounds of living, and noxious fumes lay like low-lying fog over asphalt and concrete. As if it were a world away, on this penthouse roof high above Atlanta the air was laden only with the scent of flowers and fine food. An April sun cast pools of shade beneath a profusion of ornamental trees. Lush foliage, still beaded with moisture from an early-morning misting, glittered emerald in contrast to Patrick's shorn auburn curls. The strains of a violin drifted through the garden, blending muted conversations into its music. Beyond the glass tower a clear day offered a view that seemed to reach and rise forever.

A paradise, chosen by Briggs, an adversary seeking to disarm another. But Patrick McCallum was immune to the charm of this contained garden in the sky. He thought neither of the street below nor of this haven that by night, under the star-studded sky, would be stunning.

It was midday, the sun was high and the time had come. The moment Patrick relished—the ending of a confrontation, the sweet seduction of winning. The kill.

Patrick was the consummate competitor. Icy boardroom fencing, hotheaded barroom brawl or sportsman's games, he fought hard. He fought fairly. He fought to win.

Briggs, of Briggs Publishing, was full of sly tricks. Patrick expected no less. He welcomed the challenge. The more cunning the opponent, the sweeter his victory.

In his thirty-seven years, Patrick McCallum had lost, in the boardroom, in the barroom and on the gaming field. But not in a long, long while. He did not recognize the impossible, barely understood the despair of failure. As the barbarian who fought to live, and lived to fight, he knew only the primeval excitement of success.

If, in this moment, the exhilaration was lacking, he ignored it. There would be time later to savor the victory. For now he had to think business. Briggs Publishing was his, one more acquisition for McCallum Investments, except for Briggs's last trick.

Almost languidly Patrick turned to the dark, still man seated by his side. Rafe Courtenay, CEO of McCallum American, had laid the groundwork for this deal. He knew Briggs. Patrick's look locked for an instant with Rafe's. With neither shrug nor nod a silent message passed between them.

Watch him.

Patrick swung his attention back to Briggs. His indolence did not change, nor did the lazy smile. The big body did not stir, nor the massive shoulders tense. The idle tapping ceased, as if a big, affable man had grown even more comfortable. Illusion. Beneath the veneer the poised strength was more threatening, the penetrating stare more fierce, the utter concentration more unrelenting. This was it. The kill.

Tension spilled out over the room. A silent, telepathic tidal wave disrupted the comfortable serenity as effectively as a scream. Patrick's seething quiet compelled attention. In a sudden hush the sun-washed dining room was inexplicably electrified. From the waiter, resplendent in Hungarian finery, to the bejeweled matron, every eye was drawn to Patrick.

From Patrick, to Courtenay, to Briggs, their glances darted. Something was happening. Something wickedly, deliciously gossip-worthy. Avid gazes swept the table, lingered on Rafe, dismissed Briggs, riveted on Patrick.

The violin faltered, the musician himself teetered on the vortex. After a moment he began again with a tune too lively, jarring a mesmerized hostess from her somnolence. The young woman winced, her bracelets clanking against the pitcher in her hand. Reminded of her duties, she started forward to fill Briggs's empty glass.

"No, Irina." Arthritic fingers closed about her wrist.

The young woman paused. An empty glass, a neglected cup, were cardinal sins in a dominion ruled by a gentle tyrant. Now that tyrant was saying no. "But, Grandmama," Irina protested, "the glasses."

"No." The old woman did not release her. "Stalking cats do not want interruption. Even by one so pretty."

The younger woman looked into the ancient face of Madame Zara. Beauty had faded, but wit and wisdom had not. It was evident when the tiny woman left her post at the cash register, as now, relaxing her iron vigil, moving regally through a clientele more familiar than unfamiliar. In a lighthearted mood she had passed among them, making pleasant and sometimes outrageous predictions. She did not tell fortunes. She was Magyar, Hungarian, not gypsy. Yet in her sly humor were grains of truth. Madame Zara sensed what others could not. Understood what they could only guess.

Today's sojourn had excluded one table. Regarding its occupants, she spoke in a low, accented voice. "Jungle cats, Irina, teasing an alley cat. Waiting for his fatal move."

"Jungle cats?" Irina smiled. Even for Grandmama this was too theatrical. "This is hardly a jungle."

"No matter. They carry their jungle with them." Madame Zara touched the jeweled pin over her left breast. "Here."

Irina's veneer of sophistication slipped as she realized this was not theater. What she felt—the excitement, the electrical current; what the diner felt—the awareness, the sense of the unusual; Grandmama felt more. Anticipating one of the old woman's strange stories, Irina turned toward Rafe Courtenay. "The dark one, Grandmama. What sort of cat is he?"

"Ah. The American." Black eyes snapped, taking the measure of six feet of lean, heavy-shouldered male, untamed by proper jacket, crisply creased trousers or perfect tie. "A man from the bayous, a Creole. Wild as the panther, hair black as midnight, eyes that blaze green in cold rage."

Sun sparkled over the spill of a fountain. Leaves rustled in the breeze that whispered through an open canopy. A strand of pure white hair drifted about a withered cheek.

Absently the old woman tucked it into a braid worn like a coronet. "A panther." As her whisper faded, the studied perfection of the rooftop garden was suddenly not so studied. The air was redolent with the primal scent of earth and heat. The uncivilized were here, cloaked in perfect dress. Disturbing, exciting, bringing their jungle in their hearts.

In the stillness the improbable jig of the violin intruded. The old woman drew herself from her fantasy. Retreating behind the counter, she slid onto her tall seat before the register, returning to her watch.

Drawn into her grandmother's lore, Irina wanted more. "And the other?" Patrick, brawny and imposing, filled her sight. "The big handsome one with the lovely accent?"

"That one." Madame Zara sat ramrod straight, her dark eyes on Patrick. "A Scot. Laird of his clan, ruler of all he touches. A hard man, of little gentleness. A cynic who believes in little beyond himself. He wouldn't thank you for your praise. He neither likes nor needs flattery." Her eyes grew distant as she reached deeper into her vision. "But for the panther, he is a man who needs nothing. No one. He is alone. He is one.

"One," the ancient seeress whispered. "But that one a lion."

Irina considered the sober lines of Patrick's face, the strong chin, the high, lined forehead, the mouth that rarely smiled. He was tall, with a body bigger than most, lean of hip, broad of shoulder. In passing she had heard the roll of the *R* and had seen the flash of fierce blue eyes. His hair varied in the light from red to dark auburn. And though it was closely clipped, she imagined he was a man who often forgot. Then it would grow into a mane of auburn curls. Beneath the scars that marked his lip and forehead, beneath his quiet stillness, he seemed a man of controlled strength, of barely tethered passion.

Irina shivered, feeling the rightness in her grandmama's vision, and wondered if there was a woman who could tame the lion.

Her bracelets clattered against the misted pitcher, reminding of other tables, other diners. With one last glance at two more intriguing than handsome, she hurried away.

Across the room Patrick leaned forward in lazy impatience. Oblivious of the sharp, probing interest, he spoke in a rolling burr. "No last strategy, Briggs? No final maneuver to up the ante?"

He smiled as Briggs swallowed and cleared his throat. The man had been dishonest about his company and himself, thinking he'd done what few had—outwitted Patrick McCallum and his henchman, Rafe Courtenay—taking McCallum American for more than the company was worth. In the flush of success he'd intended to try for more. Until penetrating eyes impaled him and a smiling Patrick McCallum dared him to try.

"First," Patrick continued softly, "consider your company's value to me. Its limited value."

Briggs's mouth sagged. Fear that his greed had led to a fatal mistake leapt into his eyes. His hale, ruddy skin turned sallow. His mouth and throat were parched. He reached for his water glass and found it empty.

"Ah," Patrick commiserated. "It's hard to think with a dry mouth. Perhaps we can remedy that." His stare held Briggs's a moment longer, then moved slowly away. His big body turned, seeking out the hostess. He lifted a hand to summon her, then froze.

His hand came down by increments, the summons never completed. He did not turn, nor did he move. The languid ease vanished. Rafe Courtenay, who liked nothing more than to sit back, watching Patrick move in for the kill, was instantly alert. Keenly aware of the change, his own gaze lifted, following the path that Patrick's had taken.

A young woman, her hand tucked loosely through her escort's arm, stood poised on the threshold beyond the hostess. As Rafe watched, she stepped into the sunlight that filled the restaurant. He had the fleeting impression of flowing, golden hair, sun-warmed skin, and a tall, slender figure wrapped in a dress of rich blue. A beautiful woman with a familiar face.

He shifted his attention to Patrick and was startled. Patrick hadn't moved, hadn't blinked. In all the years of a friendship begun before their teens, Rafe had never seen this look of thunderstruck awe on the face of the big Scot. Briggs was forgotten. This final sparring and the cool gratification of success, as well. Rafe knew that even he was forgotten.

"Who is she?" Patrick muttered. Rafe struggled with shock, not the name that was on the tip of his tongue, and the question became a demand. "Who is she?"

Drawn from his self-absorption, Briggs flinched, his knee hitting the table. Before Rafe could speak, he was exclaiming, "Good Lord! Jordana!"

Patrick did not react as if he'd heard. He was silent as the woman in blue moved past his table and through the room. With her hand still resting lightly in the curve of his arm, she walked with her companion beyond the fountain, beneath the foliage, from sunlight to shadow and back again into the light. Her back was straight, her breasts high. Beneath the drifting skirt of her dress, her long, lean thighs moved gracefully. The soft fabric clung and swayed, delineating the swell of a hip, the nip of her waist. She moved with confidence, her head up, her gaze straight before her. Beneath the white-gold fall of her hair, her features were serene. When the sun struck her face, no frown crinkled her eyes or marred the clean line of her forehead. As her companion spoke, she turned to him, intent on his words.

The husky sound of her laughter drifted to Patrick. It was a lovely sound.

He watched with the same brazen interest as he'd been watched. From his distant vantage he missed nothing. He saw her escort draw back her chair. He caught his breath as her long, tapered fingers slid over the wood and down the length of the back, like a sensualist who loved the touch of fine things. He noted the way her skirt settled about her, flowing over the damask seat. His gaze hardened as her escort touched her cheek, smiled, then sat across from her.

The sun had crossed beyond the meridian; the shadows it cast seemed lighter now, and the rustling leaves drew lazy patterns about her. Deliberately, every move careful, every gesture controlled, she folded her napkin over her lap, then curled her fingers about a water glass that had not yet been filled. Patiently she sat, holding the fragile crystal. Again the sensualist savoring the touch of delicate beauty.

Beyond the windowed chrysalis a cloudless sky, pallid with the white-hot brilliance of midday, began to deepen with the first hint of afternoon. Soon the blue would grow richer, deeper, matching the hue of her dress. And, Patrick wondered, her eyes?

Beneath his unblinking scrutiny, she tilted her head again, listening in rapt attention. As before, her face was serene, unmarked, until her eyes crinkled, her lips curved and her laughter floated through the room.

As if the sound had released him, he turned from her, the look of intense concentration settling over his face once more. His hard, cold focus fastened on Briggs.

Rafe settled back in his seat, still puzzled by Patrick's unusual reaction to a woman who was undeniably lovely, but ready to continue with the business at hand. In the next instant, in a great show of reaction for his impassive face, Patrick had him lifting a startled brow.

"Jordana?" Patrick prompted Briggs, as intent on the answer as moments ago when a question and its answer meant the dispersal of millions.

Briggs shrugged, his confusion plain. "Just Jordana."

"*Just* Jordana?" Patrick snapped. "What does that mean?"

"It means she's called only that. No one knows her last name. She's a mystery, a beautiful mystery."

"What the hell!" Patrick caught himself, reining in his temper. If Briggs meant to irritate him, he did it well. "She's a mystery, yet you recognized her. You were startled that she's here, yet she is. A little ambiguous, wouldn't you say?"

"Not this time," Rafe interceded, flicking a look of contempt at Briggs. "He might prefer a lie when the truth would do, but he's telling it straight. There's hardly a person in all of Atlanta who doesn't know Jordana's face. So would you, Patrick, if you spent more time here and less in Scotland. Jordana's on the cover of every magazine of any merit, and has been for months. If you'd been in the States longer than two days, you would've seen for yourself.

"She's the most sought-after model to come on the scene in a long while. No one knows who she is or where she's been all these years. I'm neither monk nor recluse and I've never seen her. No one I know has. Perhaps Jordana isn't even her real name." Rafe glanced at Jordana as she lifted the crystal goblet that had been filled. "It must've taken a pretty special occasion to bring her out of seclusion."

"Is the man her lover? Her husband?" The first, Patrick could dismiss. The latter, no. The one unbending rule in his affairs was that they were never adulterous. He'd learned early the pain of adultery, watching helplessly as his mother's had destroyed his father.

The barest frown creased Rafe's face. Patrick was jumping from A to Z with one look. The Scot was known to be impatient, but never foolish. "I have no idea who the man is."

"Find out."

"Patrick..."

Patrick cut him off with an impatient gesture. "Who does she model for?"

"I would imagine the highest bidder."

"Find out."

"Is that an order?" There was steel in the even timbre of Rafe's voice.

"Yes," Patrick said curtly. Briggs's gasp of surprise stopped the next retort. In an exasperated gesture he ran his hand through his bright curls. He'd been arrogant. Even more than was usual for the great Patrick Mc-Callum, he admitted with weary sarcasm.

Antagonizing Rafe wasn't the answer for the strange, restless boredom that plagued him. Not even Rafe, who understood him better than anyone in the world, could know that life was monotonous now. What had been exciting was now drudgery. There was no exhilaration, no fulfillment. Time and again Patrick had told himself the dissatisfaction would pass, that it was a temporary aberration, a mood, the times. He had worked harder, played harder. Sometimes at a man-killing pace. None of it worked. The zest was gone. The passion, the hallmark of his life, eluded him.

Until today.

Until the glimpse of a woman entranced him. Nothing in months had captured his interest or intrigued him as she. She was honey and sunlight in the strange dark of his life. Perhaps she was real, perhaps only illusion, the creation of a hungry, jaded mind.

He had to know and was too consumed by the need to take up the gauntlet thrown down by Rafe. For once he didn't want to duel with his friend, who was never slow in taking him to task when he overstepped himself. "No, Rafe." He smiled wryly. "It's not an order."

Rafe was startled. When Patrick was too high-handed and the icy temper of the Creole collided with the hot blood of the Scot, the Creole won more than he lost. Only because Patrick was honest enough to admit his arrogance—and only after a protracted and heated exchange. Rafe's gaze narrowed. For a long moment he studied Patrick, then he laughed. "Not an order, a strong request."

"Yeah," Patrick agreed.

Rafe nodded, the tension gone as quickly as it had come. "Just as a matter of enlightenment, where will Maeve fit in this little triangle?"

"She won't." Patrick dismissed his paramour of six months as easily as he would've discarded a worn shirt.

"I don't think Maeve Delmari will absent herself from your life quite as readily as you intend."

Patrick shrugged. "She knew the rules."

"She knew your rules. I suspect she had a different set for herself."

"Doesn't matter. We agreed that when the affair was over either of us could walk away with no explanation.

That's what I'm doing. What I should've done weeks ago." Patrick had been weary of Maeve for some time. Because he was equally weary of the emptiness that followed the ending of a liaison, he let this one drag on long past its prime. Another mistake created by his strange ennui.

"She's been expecting you since you flew in from Scotland, Patrick. She's attached some special significance to this trip."

"Her mistake."

"Yes," Rafe mused, remembering the look on Patrick's face, his incredible reaction to Jordana. "I suppose it was."

"Have your secretary call the jeweler tomorrow. Maeve likes red. Send her something in rubies."

"Sure, it's the color of blood," Rafe drawled, but said no more. He didn't want to argue the point. Just as he didn't want to be present when the volatile Maeve received Patrick's farewell in rubies. "Just for my own information, Patrick, what if this man with Jordana is her lover?"

"What if he is?" Patrick dismissed the man as easily as he had Maeve Delmari.

"Then let me phrase it this way. What if Jordana prefers her life as it is?"

Beyond Rafe, Jordana was constantly in Patrick's sight. She was alone now, her escort having disappeared into the private regions of the restaurant, which housed a bank of telephones. She sat quietly, a solitary island of irresistible calm. Sliding back his chair, Patrick rose, casting a look at the dazed Briggs and a sardonically amused Rafe. "What better time than the present to find out?"

Every head in the room turned to follow him. Even the most circumspect abandoned the pretext of disinterest.

They were too well-bred to approach, but not to watch. This was too delicious. A double coup—the incomparable Patrick McCallum and the elusive Jordana in the same room. And from Patrick's manner, locked on a collision course.

With a quiet tread Patrick wound his way through the room, deaf to murmured comments, blind to wistful feminine glances. At the table farthest from the crowd, he stopped. His mind registered that Jordana wore absolutely no jewelry as he waited for her to acknowledge him. When she didn't react, he called her name, the curling consonants giving it the sound of a rippling brook.

He waited an eternity, until her eyes lifted, searching, finding his. He'd been wrong to presume they would be simply blue. But could they really be amethyst?

Her stare, strange and alluring, looked through him. No flicker of emotion or response crossed her composed features. "I'm sorry, do I know you?"

Her voice was as pleasing as Patrick expected. "No. But you will."

"I beg your pardon?" A frown drew a fine line between her brows.

"Before we're done, Jordana, you'll know me very well," he promised softly.

There was alarm now on her face, in her voice. "You're mistaken, Mr...."

"McCallum, but from you I prefer Patrick."

She made no nervous gestures, none of the coy, flirtatious moves he expected. Instead, she folded her hands, yet the punishing grip of her ringless fingers betrayed her. "You're mistaken, Mr. McCallum, you won't be anything to me. Not anything at all."

"The mistake is yours, Jordana."

"What the hell is this?" Jordana's companion insinuated himself between them, rounding on Patrick. "Who the devil are you?"

"No, Philip." Jordana's fingers closed over the smaller man's hand as it rested on her shoulder. "The gentleman has simply made a mistake. He mistook me for a friend." Those dark amethyst eyes looked vaguely in Patrick's direction. "Or was it a lover, Mr. McCallum?"

Patrick's gaze deliberately dropped to the fullness of her breasts, lingering long on the delicate rise barely visible beneath the open drape of her dress. "We both know the answer to that. Or we will very soon."

His answer, murmured on a half breath, accomplished what his wicked looks could not. Her face flamed, and her hand gripped Philip's even harder. Yet her voice was level; not even the most avid listener would find anything amiss in her tone. "No, Mr. . . ."

"Patrick."

". . . McCallum," she continued. "We know now."

"And what is it that *we* know, love?"

Those amethyst eyes were on him, dismissing him as if they did not see him. "We know that we are *not* friends, that we will *never* be lovers, and my name is not *love.*"

"Never is a long time," Patrick said as he grinned. "And 'love' suits you infinitely well."

"Philip!" Jordana's hand lifted from Philip's in a gesture that silenced his retort. "I'd like to leave now." Her hand remained as it was, half-raised, waiting as he struggled with his outrage. After a moment she said, "Please, Philip."

"All right, Dani." Philip sighed, breaking his stare with Patrick. He clasped her outstretched hand and, as her fingers twined about his, guided her to her feet.

Patrick remained as he was, blocking the way. Then, as those cool, wonderful eyes stared right past him, he stepped aside. She had dismissed him so completely she truly did not see him. A rare sense of doubt jarred him as she stepped by, leaving him enveloped in her floral scent as Philip led her from the room.

"Sunlight and flowers," he murmured. "Exactly what I need." Jordana vanished before he turned back to his table.

Briggs had fled, the deal settled with Rafe in favor of McCallum American. Patrick felt the old exhilaration rising, but it had far more to do with the mysterious Jordana than with Briggs.

In answer to Rafe's questioning look, Patrick said simply, "Find her. Begin with the man. His name is Philip."

Rafe nodded and gathered up the check. "She must be quite a lady to inspire such loyalty in her...ah...friend. I think the little fellow would've fought you."

"Little?"

"Patrick, everyone is little compared to you."

Patrick wasn't listening. "I'd forgotten what it was like to feel so alive. She's beautiful, Rafe, and at the moment she thinks she hates my guts."

"Maybe she does."

Patrick smiled. "Then helping her change her mind should make it all the more interesting, shouldn't it?"

Rafe wanted to caution his friend, but it was too late. When challenged, Patrick was ruthless and impetuous, but never quite like this. The Creole knew that trying to stop him now would be like stepping in front of a freight train. What Patrick wanted, he went after. Whether he would get it this time remained to be seen.

Patrick was halfway out the door, his head filled with the memory of long, caressing fingers and dark amethyst eyes, when Rafe joined him. Madame Zara's bright scrutiny followed them, one tall and dark, the other massive and fiery. Men who, for an afternoon, had turned her peaceful garden into a jungle.

"The lion thinks to tame the woman, but it is he who will be tamed...by that most wonderful of all things," she murmured. "A tiger's heart cloaked in gentleness."

Then, smiling a pleased smile, Madame Zara turned away.

Two

"Well, now, how about them apples?" Miranda Taylor stared at the telephone, engrossed in a sudden flood of questions. A manicured nail tapped a staccato beat against the receiver, and a frown narrowed her eyes as she looked past the understated elegance of the room to the walled courtyard beyond. Then, with a shrug, returning the instrument to its place, she rose from the rose silk sofa.

Her stride was long, the gliding, confident step of a beautiful woman. At a small bar she splashed sparkling water into two stemmed glasses and, cradling them in her palms, walked through an open French door into the sun.

The sound of flowing water and the scent of blooming things mingling with heat and light greeted her. Intent as she was on her purpose, the tranquillity escaped her. By a chaise lounge drawn near the pool she stopped.

"You lie out here much longer, Jordana Daniel, your skin's going to be black as mine. Then Philip will complain. Anyway, suntans are passé." The last was added even though she knew the seminude woman who basked in the sun cared nothing for style or suntans. As with everything, it was the sensation, the aura, the touch of heat and light on her skin.

In a sensual move Jordana rolled to a sitting position, lifting her face to the sun, savoring it for another moment. "Has it been that long, Randy?"

"Long enough." Then relenting, she added, "But not too long." Snagging a shirt from the table by the lounge, she dropped it in Jordana's lap. "Just in case."

Accustomed to Randy's scolding, Jordana chuckled as she slipped into the shirt, carefully buttoning it from neck to hip, covering her bare breasts and the miniscule bikini bottom. "There. All buttoned up, prim and proper."

"I swear, in another life you must have been nature's child, wild and free, roaming some tropical island without a stitch."

And that, Randy thought as she eyed Jordana's mane of white-gold hair tumbling from the ribbon that caught it haphazardly at her crown, was exactly why her image was on the cover of nearly every magazine. Jordana's face turned heads. She was unstudied beauty and freedom and joy to the millions who gazed at her pictures. They looked at her and smiled. And remembered. Jordana was the embodiment of forgotten dreams. The gentle hope of the future. The passion of new love. Her image shone out from the glossy covers and coaxed an answering smile from the grimmest of the grim. That, more than the mystery, was her charisma.

"Randy, have you considered Philip's suggestion?"

"What suggestion?" Randy knew very well what suggestion. Philip Conroy wasn't satisfied with the success Jordana had brought to his faltering career. Now he wanted to draw her into it. As he explained it, he wanted to complement light with dark. Contrasting her sultry worldliness against Jordana's wholesome charm.

Two faces of sensuality. The carnal. The undefiled.

Eros and innocence.

"You know what question," Jordana said mildly as Randy took her hand, folding her fingers about the stem of the glass. She sipped from it gratefully before she continued. "The modeling."

"I've thought about it," Randy quipped as she sank into the lounge beside Jordana's. "Just long enough to know it's the last thing I want. I've made my living with my face and my body. Once was enough, thank you."

"This would be different."

"Everything's different from the life," Randy said bluntly.

"Don't." Jordana's hand jerked, spilling sparkling water over it. "The past is done. Neither of us is what we were."

"Thanks to you."

"No." Jordana stretched out her hand, waiting for Randy's, then clasped it in a quick, affectionate gesture and released it. "Thanks to both of us." She was completely oblivious to the uniqueness of their relationship. For Jordana they were not black or white, wealthy or poor, wanton or defective. Ten years ago, running from humiliation and repression, she'd set her life on a collision course with Randy's. What had begun poorly on a squalid street ended well, and they were simply friends. "I only mentioned Philip's idea because it occurred to me you might want more than *this*."

This was serving as Jordana's traveling companion, her secretary, her housekeeper, and managing the affairs of a small recording venture she'd launched years ago. When there were modeling assignments, it meant doing her makeup, her hair, or even choosing her costume.

"There's no more I want than a quiet life and time to raise my daughter." Tracing her finger over the rim of her glass, she watched the scintillating liquid. "Unless you think I should do more to earn my keep."

"More!" Jordana's laugh blended into the hush of the garden. "If you did any more, I couldn't afford you."

Randy smiled at the compliment. Jordana was wealthy by any standard. Some of it inherited, some earned by her own initiative and, if she wished, by the small recording company she'd founded. More had been added to the coffer of late by her modeling. That Jordana counted her of more value than that vast amount set Randy's concern at ease. "I matter that much to you?" she asked simply because she wanted the words.

"You matter. But if you wanted to accept . . ."

"I don't," Randy said, putting the matter to rest. "Speaking of Philip, he called earlier. It's definite. Chassen wants you for their Summer Girl."

"Girl," Jordana scoffed. "I'm twenty-eight. How will we manage that?"

"For one thing, you don't look more than twenty. For another, according to Philip they're looking for a mood more than an age and the shots will be alfresco. His word, not mine. And he has Chassen's approval to begin here."

"No traveling? Terrific!"

"Not to mention that this is the big plum Philip's wanted. What he was after when he traded on your friendship to persuade you to model for him."

"He's kept his word, Randy. I've never had to deal with anyone other than Philip. No one knows who I am, nor what I'm like."

"That brings up another point. Philip says this guy who's been looking for you hasn't given up."

"Patrick."

Something in Jordana's tone had Randy turning to stare at her. Patrick! Not Who? or Mr. McCallum. Simply Patrick. What did she hear in that name? Fear, exasperation, interest? "Not him—the other one. Courtenay. According to gossip, McCallum's gone home."

"To Scotland," Jordana said, and wondered why the sound of his softly accented voice still lingered in her mind.

"Yeah, to Scotland. But the man's persistent. He hasn't given up."

"He's a proud man, accustomed to women falling at his feet. I didn't. When his pride heals, he'll forget."

"I'm not so sure."

"I am."

"You're an expert on men all of a sudden?" Randy's tone was droll, gently mocking.

"Hardly." In all her twenty-eight years there had never been a man in Jordana's life. No puppy love, no teenage infatuation, nor even a collegiate fling. Perhaps a man to love, to share with, would be the normal course for a normal woman, but she was contented as she was. A contentment hard won, and she had no desire to change it.

Patrick McCallum had been no more than a beguiling voice in a sunlit restaurant. Arrogant, confident, making bold assumptions and provocative promises. Yes, provocative. No man had intrigued and disturbed her as Patrick McCallum had. His arrogance, his confidence, had sent her on a headlong flight from the restaurant and ultimately from Atlanta.

Only when she was tucked safely away in her small estate on the colonial coast of Georgia had she put the man and the encounter into perspective. "Everything we've read about him describes him as a womanizer who plays fast and loose. I caught his fancy for a moment. But that's all it was. A passing fancy. There'll be others. If there aren't already."

"My, my, my." Randy shook her head at Jordana's ability to ignore the obvious. "Listen to the woman talk trash. Passing fancy? Ha! The man's obsessed. He's going to stay obsessed until he finds you and has what he wants."

"And what is that, Randy?"

"Honey, even you aren't that innocent. He wants *you!* Body and soul."

"Why?"

"Only God and Patrick McCallum know that. But if I was a gambling lady, I'd lay odds that women have always been too easy for him. Maybe he's bored, and you're a challenge." Consciously sliding into the language of her past, she drawled, "And let me tell you, sugar, there ain't nothing that gets a man's blood pumping faster than a challenge."

"There are other challenges out there."

"Lots. None of them is you. Just be prepared."

"Prepared for what?"

"That's something else only Mr. McCallum knows." Randy glanced up at the sun, judging the time. "If you stay out here any longer, your nose will be pink and Philip will scream bloody murder. Cassie's due home from camp in an hour. Enough time to make chocolate-chip cookies. Want to help?"

There was nothing Cassie loved more than chocolate-chip cookies and no one Jordana loved more than Cassie, Randy's nine-year-old daughter. She was laughing as she rose. "I get to lick the beater."

"We'll compromise," Randy decreed. "One beater for you, one for me. The bowl for Cassie."

"Done."

Trespass. The invasion of the property or rights of another without consent.

And this was trespass, Patrick admitted as he stepped into a walled garden where ferns and flowers grew about a rock-lined pool. Jordana Daniel's retreat was exclusive, secluded and charming. When Rafe had summoned him from Scotland, saying simply that Jordana had been found, he had little idea what to expect. Given that he knew now that she was heiress to most of the fortune of Henry Daniel, financier and entrepreneur, he would've thought a mansion and fences complete with guards. Instead, he'd found a modest home encompassed by sprawling grounds, and beyond this garden not a wall in sight.

"Walk right in, Patrick. Make yourself at home," he muttered with an edge of disgust in his voice. It was too late for conscience. He'd gone too far to back down. All because a beautiful woman had looked straight through him, her cool amethyst eyes challenging him as he'd never been challenged before.

Those eyes haunted him, day and night. Even his beloved Scotland offered no respite. But today marked the beginning of an exorcism.

Taking the path that led from the pool, he found himself at the back of the house. At the kitchen to be exact, occupied by a woman who was hardly what he expected.

She was black and trim and gorgeous. When he tapped on the door frame, she looked up from the carrots she was cutting. Without missing a beat, she said, "Mr. McCallum, what kept you?"

"You were expecting me?"

"Sooner or later." Wiping her fingers on a towel, she came to meet him with her hand outstretched. "I'm Randy Taylor, Jordana's secretary, companion, friend, whatever."

"You knew I would come?" Patrick took her hand, liking its firm grip.

"When Philip told us you were looking for Jordana, I made it my business to find out about you. Everything I learned said you never give up until you get what you want. At the moment you think you want Jordana."

"Would I be correct in assuming from your greeting that you don't think my intrusion in her life is a bad idea?"

"What you should assume is that I'm bowing to the inevitable and reserving judgment. Jordana does need someone in her life. Someone other than my daughter and Philip and me. The only way that will happen is with a man like you. One who takes matters into his own hands, who can break the barriers she's built around herself." Taking back her hand, Randy rested her fists on her hips. With her eyes narrowed she studied him carefully. "You may be the right man, you may not. There are difficulties you don't anticipate. When you encounter them, we'll see if you've got the guts to stick."

Guts? Patrick was amused and curious. Why would this extraordinary woman who hadn't turned a hair when a strange man appeared in her kitchen think he needed guts? "Difficulties? Does Miss Daniel have six fingers on each hand? A wooden leg?"

"No extra fingers, or toes. Her legs are perfect."

"From what I saw, she's perfect all over."

"Then you're as blind as..." Randy turned away. Going to the counter, she picked up a carrot. "If you're still here at six, you're welcome to stay for dinner, Mr. McCallum. We dine early, for my daughter." With a jut of her chin she added, "Follow your nose past the pool and the brook. You'll find Jordana in the meadow with Philip."

"Just like that?"

"Just like that."

"No announcement. No warning for Jordana?"

"Nope."

"Why?"

"Because everything I've learned about you tells me that beneath your arrogance and aggression—and your womanizing—you're a decent human being."

"It does?" Patrick lifted a sardonic brow.

"I read a lot. As much between the lines as on them. I don't know what you had for breakfast this morning, but I know everything else that matters."

"I assume you ran a Dun and Bradstreet?"

"Of course."

"For your employer."

"For my friend."

"You're putting a lot of faith into what you read."

And in what I hear in Jordana's voice when she speaks of you, Randy thought. "In what I read. In my own judgment. I've a lifetime of experience in judging men."

"A lifetime." Patrick's look swept over her, noting her youth.

"Lifetimes can be lived in a year, a month, a day."

"I see." He let the matter drop, but he would have an explanation. Later. "You could be wrong. I could hurt her."

"I know. Some gambles you take. I wouldn't have thrown her in your path, but now that you're here, I won't stop you." She couldn't if she tried.

"If you lose your gamble and I do hurt her?"

"If it's deliberate, I'll cut your heart out." Randy lifted the vegetable scraper with a wry look that turned instantly serious. "Never doubt it. Once this hand was more accustomed to a switchblade than kitchen utensils."

"I see," Patrick said softly, but he didn't. He didn't understand anything about any of this. Not about himself, nor the effect the mysterious Jordana had on him, nor this strange, lovely woman who welcomed in one breath and threatened with another. He didn't understand, but he would. Oh yes, he would. It would be part of the exorcism. "Follow my nose? Past the pool, by the brook to the meadow?"

"You got it, Mr. McCallum."

"Patrick."

"You got it, Patrick," Randy repeated with the ghost of a grin.

When he had gone, she dropped the tool and the vegetable into the sink. Gripping the edge of the counter, she closed her eyes, praying she hadn't just made the mistake of her life.

"Okay, Dani. Just run toward the lake. Twelve paces or so. Stop, turn. Fling your hair about so that it swirls across your face. You're a kid. Eighteen. It's summer, you love it."

"Eighteen." Jordana laughed, and the husky sound of it drifted to the small copse of trees where Patrick stood.

"This is a dreamy sequence—we're using soft focus. Not that you need it. Later we'll go into sharp, true edges. This is about time and passages and moods. Summer's new and fresh, and you're the Summer Girl. You'll mature together. Now, ready?"

At Jordana's nod, Philip put his hands on her shoulders, turning her toward the lake. When he leaned to kiss her cheek, Patrick felt the surge of irrational irritation. He'd scoured the countryside for her, waited weeks for this day. He wanted it to be his hands on her shoulders. His lips at her cheek, on her mouth.

In time it would be.

Once, twice, three times they went through the routine, and each time Philip Conroy put his hands on her. At every excuse he put his hands on her. Seething with rage he knew he had no right to feel, Patrick gripped the trunk of a small sapling and wondered how much more he could stand. He watched as Jordana made one more run down the hill, stopping just short of the lake. When Conroy drew her back, she was only inches away from the steep banks that dropped sharply to water so deep it glittered like a dark sapphire in the sun.

The lake, the sky and the meadow that surrounded them were vivid with the newness of spring. In contrast to the brightness, Jordana was dressed in a frock of some sheer, white fluttering material. The only color in her costume was the collage of multicolored cabbage roses circling the brim of a white straw hat she carried.

Begrudgingly Patrick admitted that Conroy was superb at creating the mood he wanted. What he'd drawn from Jordana was an aura of youth. Innocent youth, like the first day of summer, trembling on the brink of life. Patrick didn't doubt that every man who saw the resulting pictures would feel as he did. Captivated. His own dreams mingling with desire for her. A sweet, delicious ache in the center of him.

"That's it for the day," Philip called out abruptly. "The light's changing. If we have what I think we do, later we'll go for a different mood. Still soft, still gentle, but dreamy. Our innocent young girl whose life is perfect will begin to daydream about what it could be. We're going through this maturing process gradually." Philip hesitated, throwing an arm about her shoulders as if he wanted to hold her while he said the rest. "I've got a call out now for male models. One to play the lover in the last sequence."

"No!" Jordana dodged away from his embrace. "You know I never work with anyone but you."

"Honey, you have to this time. A lover's a natural progression for what we're looking for."

"No!" The desperate edge in the single word raised Patrick's hackles like the rasp of a ragged nail. He heard more than anger or surprise. He heard panic.

"Jordana." Philip reached for her. "It has to be this way. I didn't tell you at first because . . ."

"No."

"Jordana, please."

"You heard the lady, Conroy. She said no!"

"Patrick!" Jordana whirled toward the sound of his voice, her trouble with Philip forgotten.

"McCallum!" Philip exclaimed in unison with her. "How the devil did you get here?"

"By plane, by car and by foot." Patrick dismissed Conroy without a glance as he moved farther into the meadow. He was too pleased by the sound of his name on Jordana's lips, his hungry gaze too filled by her, to bother with Conroy.

"This is a closed set. All Jordana's locations are closed and secret." Philip was babbling, surprised at seeing the huge Scot advancing on him. "Nobody was to know. Nobody did know except . . . Richard Chassen! This is his project. He knew. You or your henchman, Courtenay, got to him."

"It doesn't matter what I know or from whom, Conroy. What matters is that I'm here and you're leaving."

"If you think for one minute that I'm going to leave you here alone with Jordana, you'd better think again," Philip blustered, though, taking into account Patrick's size, coupled with his reputation, opposing him would be like lying down before a steamroller, daring it to run over him.

"It's all right, Philip." Jordana hadn't moved or turned her face from the intruder. She didn't turn to Philip now as she urged him to do as Patrick demanded. Her thoughts were scattered and her nerves taut. Though she'd identified him immediately by his voice, he was still a stranger. Beneath the surface a very angry stranger. She had to be crazy to put herself in his care, but he'd gotten past Randy. In fact, Randy had to have sent him; that was a vote of trust. Later, when she'd done what she had to do—what her wise, loyal friend obviously thought she should do alone—she would find out what quality prompted that trust. "Go on along. I'm sure Randy's waiting. Tell her Mr. McCallum found us and that we'll be along later."

"I think I should stay, Dani."

"Mr. McCallum isn't a madman, Philip. If he were, with a word Randy would've set off every alarm system on the grounds. You aren't a madman, are you, Mr. McCallum?"

"If I were, I would hardly admit it." And if I were, he wondered, would I know it myself? Considering the here and now, he wondered. He truly wondered.

"In any case it's too late now." Jordana drew a deep breath and put herself completely in his hands. "You have work to do, Philip, and our visitor will see me back to the house."

Another facet of her mystical appeal. Trust and elusiveness. A combination that set a man's head spinning, keeping him off balance. Drawing him to her, yet dancing beyond his reach.

Patrick wanted to catch her gaze to keep her that way, if no other. But that marvelous gaze eluded him, looking toward him, never at him. The same raw urges that aloofness had triggered before were rising in him now. The arrogant need that wanted to draw her body hard against his own and kiss her until she was as senseless and hurting as he. Until those marvelous eyes saw him, really saw him, and were filled with the same desire.

A rueful look ghosted over her face, then was gone. Her voice was suddenly husky with a hidden disquiet. "You will see me back to the house, won't you, Mr. Mc-Callum?"

Swallowing the angry passion knotting his throat, he nodded. "It would be my pleasure to see Miss Daniel home."

"Jordana?" Philip tried once more. "You're sure?"

"I'm sure." Without turning to him, she put out her hand, waiting until Philip took it. "We won't be long."

When Philip had gone, with more than one backward look, Patrick smiled, a cynical quirking of his lips. Jordana hadn't moved or turned away. She stood starkly erect, her arms at her side, her fingers curling loosely into her palms. She appeared totally guileless and almost had him believing she was the Summer Girl. Innocent, uncomplicated, untried.

Almost. No one that innocent could stand before an unwelcome marauder so unperturbed. Her momentary edge of misgiving had been just that—only momentary, and only for effect. The boundaries of his cynicism expanded, grew keener, more acute, cutting with a razor's edge.

His smile was still in place, a caricature. "You really are a cool one, aren't you?"

"Am I?" Her head lifted a little, but beyond that small hint of movement there was no other reaction.

"And a good little actress, too."

"An actress? What do you base that on?"

"You spend weeks running from me. Or pretending to, and now that I'm here you hardly bat an eye." A newborn suspicion leapt into his mind. Something he hadn't considered. Had he been too blinded by his distraction to see a tactic meant to make him react exactly as he had? "Was that the idea?"

He began to circle her, moving over the meadow floor, speaking as he went. "You aren't what I'm accustomed to. You didn't react as I expected. I love a challenge, a dare. You are both."

Jordana was turning in place, following the sound of his voice, forgetting to keep herself oriented. "You think I deliberately set out to be a dare? Knowing you find them irresistible?"

"Something like that." He was still moving, his eyes on her, taking in the lines of her body, feeling his own tighten in response. If his accusations were true, then, dammit, she did it well. All of it. The dare, the enticement. The desire. He wanted her even if she were a schemer.

"How could I do that?"

Patrick lifted his hand, brushing a tousled curl from her shoulder, letting it run through his fingers like liquid sunlight. "Jordana Daniel. The golden woman. Beautiful, mysterious, aloof."

With his thumb he traced a line across her cheek. When she stood woodenly beneath his touch, his anger moved to another plane, his need to a new dimension. He wanted her to flinch, to tremble, to respond. The edge of his nail teased at the corner of her mouth, tugged at her full lower lip, then glided in an achingly slow motion over the cleft of her chin and down her neck to the pulse that throbbed at the base of her throat. Only there did he find evidence of the effect of his marauding trespass. Only then did her golden spiked lashes sweep her cheeks, shielding the violet glitter of her eyes.

"Jordana Daniel," he muttered. "Sunlight in darkness. Gentleness in a world gone mad. Elusive, exciting. Illusion, contradiction. More desirable than any woman I've ever known. It's madness but how could I resist? Could any man?"

As his hand curved about the nape of her neck, drawing her to him, he felt her shiver, heard the rhythm of her breathing quicken as her breasts brushed against the hard wall of his chest. As one hand molded their bodies, the other grasped her hair tugging back her head even as he was bending from his great height.

Her hands were at his chest, curled, passive. Her lips were soft and yielding as his teased over them. A cry, a tangle of protest and pleasure, borne on a sigh whispered over his cheek.

Illusion. Contradiction. But God, how he wanted her!

His kiss deepened, probing and thrusting. Recognizing no resistance, accepting none. Desire that had tugged at him with the claws of a lazy kitten ripped with the power of a lion. This one, he thought in a moment of sanity, would cost him far more than diamonds and rubies.

"Whatever it costs," he murmured. Knowing it would be more than money, he let his hand slide from her hair.

"Cost?" With an effort Jordana drew away. Away from the storm that caught her in its white-hot ferocity. That flared at the touch of his hand in her hair and spiraled upward with the teasing caress of his fingers. A kiss, and the madness, as he called it, was complete.

Madness of substance. With a name.

Patrick.

A voice she'd remembered in the darkness of her dreams. A hard, unyielding body that was all too real. A kiss, begun in frustration, in the end incredibly gentle.

He was bold, brash, unlike anyone she'd ever known. Unlike anyone who had ever touched her. Many men in one.

Patrick of Atlanta. Intruding, making beautiful, frightening promises.

Patrick, here. Trespassing, with strange, ugly accusations.

Patrick, who kissed her. Awakening desire, speaking only of cost.

The storm ebbed. Passion lay like a cold stone inside her. Struggling from the prison of her personal darkness, she lifted her face to a stranger. Her look was tight and grim as she moved from his embrace.

He resisted, but to keep her would have meant to hurt her. At his worst, Patrick would not inflict physical pain on one smaller, weaker. A woman. As his arms dropped away, releasing her, she stepped beyond his reach.

"Cost, Mr. McCallum?" Her voice was husky, taut and suddenly hurting.

"You called me Patrick before. I like it when you call me Patrick."

"What cost, Mr. McCallum?" Inexorable, undeterred.

"The cost to have you, Jordana Daniel." His voice was silky as he found footing on familiar ground. "What else?"

"Randy said you were arrogant." Jordana's voice failed her. The words were barely more than a whisper.

"Arrogant?" Patrick laughed, not a pretty sound. "Is it arrogant to know that you liked my kiss, that you wanted it? That you want it again?"

"No." She was backing away, sensing that as she did he was advancing.

"Yes."

Because she'd been turning, following the sound of his voice, she was completely disoriented. But that was forgotten as she turned to flee. Everything was forgotten except her need to run. To escape him.

"Jordana! Stop! Jordana!" His cry died as he lunged after her in a ground-eating stride. Catching her by the arm, he spun her roughly into his embrace as her foot slipped over the rim of the embankment.

"Damn you!" His chest heaved violently against her as he held her to him. "Are you blind?"

Her answer was muffled against the folds of his shirt, but he heard. With a terrible sense of dread coiling deeply inside him, he heard.

"What!" The word was reflexive as he put her from him. He didn't want to hear it again, but he steeled himself, knowing he would.

"Yes, Patrick." Her voice was low, matter-of-fact. She lifted her face to his. "I'm blind."

His hands jolted upward savagely, but when they framed her face they were gentle. He was as still as stone, staring into her empty gaze. The truth, the only truth that made any sense, rocked him, and so many things fell into place.

Those magnificent eyes, eyes that had looked past him, driving him to madness, had never seen him at all.

The world as Patrick McCallum knew it crumbled. His arrogant accusations lay like dust at his feet as he gathered her to him. He rocked her against him, his lips in her hair, his hands holding her as if she would break.

With the rough edge of regret in his voice he held her, murmuring, "I'm sorry, Jordana. Dear heaven, I'm sorry."

Three

———

"**Y**ou set me up."

"No." Randy tipped the decanter, poured a generous brandy, then slid it over the kitchen counter to Patrick. "You set yourself up. I just didn't try to stop you."

"You could have warned me."

"I warned you."

Difficulties.

Running a hand over the shadow of his beard, Patrick stared beyond the open doors. In the garden, flowers swayed and nodded in the breeze. From a secret nest a mockingbird sang the same sweet notes over and over again. And in a summer meadow Patrick saw Jordana.

Jordana, still, calm, her eyes, magnificent in the sun, never meeting his.

Jordana, turning in place, following the sound of his voice. Impassive beneath his kiss. Suddenly, incredibly, responding.

And then desire.

Exquisite. Soothing. With nothing of lust, nor frenzy, nor power. Only desire, as he'd never known it. Tenderness and promise, and more. Hope, dreams. Faith. The very things he'd scoffed at.

He hadn't understood what had driven him since the first time he'd seen her. He hadn't understood in the meadow, until he kissed her. Then he knew it was simply that he must have her and all she represented. He must ease himself with her, wrap himself in her golden promise.

Later, when the excitement was lost, the gold tarnished, he would walk away.

But it was not later, nor was it he who walked away.

Jordana, enchanting in the summer day, with his kiss still warm on her lips.

Jordana, slipping away to an elusive place within herself. Shutting him out. Accepting the lash of his bitterness, the ugliness of his frustration. Afraid only when he threatened to touch her again.

Jordana! Retreating. Fleeing. Fleeing from him.

Jordana, fragile and trembling in his arms, teetering at the edge of the lake. The lake she couldn't see.

Jordana! He wanted to put her from his mind, but she was with him constantly. In every thought, every memory.

His face was bleak as he looked to Randy. "Difficulties?" A shudder shook him. "Dear God, Randy!"

She saw the conflict that was tearing him apart, but was remorseless. She had set him up. Deliberately, perhaps cruelly. That much was true. But if he stuck?

Patrick McCallum wanted Jordana badly enough to cross an ocean for her. Not the usual passing fancy. Not the usual man. Jordana needed a man in her life. An unusual man. So maybe, just maybe.

"Drink this." Randy edged the brandy a fraction closer. "Jordana will be down in a few minutes." She shrugged and sighed. In for a penny, in for a pound. She'd made the play, might as well follow through. Backing down when she thought she was right wasn't her style. When she hoped she was right, she added with a prayer, "You can apologize for the minor inconvenience and leave."

In a change so subtle she hardly moved a muscle, Randy's posture changed and her tone. In a flicker of an eye the poised gentlewoman became the woman of the streets, the hardened creature with no illusions, who could mock and goad with a word or a look. "That is what you're going to do, isn't it?" Her words were smug, canny. Scorn, unmistakable in her lazy drawl. "The great Patrick McCallum is going to run."

Patrick's head was flung back. His hair, grown longer in his weeks in Scotland, brushed over his shoulders like dancing fire. There was fire in his eyes, as well, cold blue fire. Any man who had dared what Randy dared would have been sent flying by one of the Scot's brutal fists. Yet it was more than gender that kept his seething violence leashed. With grudging respect he recognized her as an uncommon adversary, one of great courage and extraordinary loyalty.

Rare qualities that leashed the beast more than her mocking. His anger was tempered, but still no little thing. Lesser foes would have retreated. Not Randy, who matched him stare for stare, the mocking question hanging between them.

Locked in combat, neither heard the grate of a light step nor saw the shadowy figure in the doorway.

The silent battle of wills continued, stretching to the breaking point. With a sharp hissing breath, Patrick was the first to look away.

"Dammit, woman!" His fist crashed on the counter with a force that threatened to shatter it. Randy didn't flinch. Patrick had never before been called a coward, nor as coolly. Not by a woman half his size. Not by anyone. A muscle flickered in his jaw as he wondered what it was she wanted and why it was so important to her. His voice was dangerously soft. "What the hell would you have me do?"

"What you came to do."

"What I . . . Have you lost your mind? The woman's blind!"

"So?" Randy's glittering, ebony stare did not waver. With a look she turned his every thought back at him to tear at him. The censure missing in Jordana when he'd finally taken her hand and walked in silence with her to the house blasted him now like a furnace.

In a gesture that was as much exasperation as anger, Patrick pushed the untouched brandy away. He needed a clear head, not alcoholic glibness. Opening his mouth, he started to speak, then shook his head mutely.

Lifting the glass he'd refused to her lips, Randy watched him over its rim. Offering neither clemency nor reprieve, she sipped, swallowed, felt the amber liquid curl through her like smoke, steadying fraying nerves. She sipped again and waited.

"Look, Randy," Patrick began impatiently, "I came in here, running roughshod over all of you. I admit it. But I didn't know. I couldn't know." He lifted his hands, fingers splayed, then, having no idea what to do with them or what more to say, he let them drop on the counter. He rarely excused or explained himself—he rarely felt the need—and he was doing it badly.

"You came wanting Jordana." Randy went bluntly for the jugular. "And by your own admission, you didn't much care who you had to step on to get her."

Patrick smothered an oath, drew a deep breath, held it and felt the calm he reached for escape him. "Yes!" he snapped, skirting the fringes of full-blown rage that threatened again. She was goading him, fueling his temper with his own arrogance, stripping away any illusion. For the first time in a long while, he didn't like what he saw. Truth hurt. It had before. It would again.

He drew a second breath, as a drowning man would his last. "Yes," he admitted almost wearily. "I came wanting Jordana. So damn cocky I thought I could make her want me just as much. I didn't care what anyone else had to say about the matter. I meant to have her."

Randy set the glass aside, folding her arms, her hidden hands clutching her sides. "Then what?"

"Then the relationship, or the infatuation, if you want to call it that, would run its course."

"Its course?" Like flu, or mumps. Only less inconvenient. Hugging her arms closer to her body, she asked the only question that mattered. "And now?"

"There is no now."

Randy's heart sank. She'd gambled and lost. Patrick was a hard man. Immutable. Astute. He might be caught off guard once, rarely twice, as with Jordana. But certainly not a third time, not by Randy Taylor, and not by the wiles of a veteran of the street. There was nothing she could do to stop him from walking out of Jordana's life.

And maybe he should.

Maybe he was too tough, too uncompromising. If he stayed, Jordana's sheltered existence would change, and he would surely hurt her. But some hurts were worth their price. Randy had Cassie as proof of that.

Jordana needed more in her life than her work and a few selected friends. She needed a man. One like Patrick. Tough, uncompromising, whose love, if it came to that, would be equally uncompromising. Who would not honor the reclusiveness that had gradually deepened in recent months.

Jordana, who'd had to be so brave, was steadily withdrawing without ever having lived.

But not if I can stop it, Randy thought with another wave of stubborn determination. She would never have created these circumstances, but now that Patrick was here, she would not give up so easily.

"You met a woman and something in her touched you. So much that you moved heaven and earth to find her. She's still that woman, the woman who brought you from the other side of the world." Randy reached for the glass. It was empty. Gripping the edge of the counter instead, she struggled to keep her voice steady. "Being blind doesn't make her less beautiful. Or less desirable."

"Perhaps to Patrick it does." Jordana spoke from the doorway.

Patrick spun the bar stool about, his elbow sending the glass tumbling. There was no splintering crash, thanks to Randy's quick reflexes, but he wouldn't have known if there were. His eyes had found Jordana, raking her over from head to toe, searching for the differences that had eluded him before.

He found them now, only because he knew.

They made her no less beautiful, no less desirable. She had changed from the white gown to a scarlet sundress that tied at her nape, leaving her shoulders bare. Her hair tumbled down her back, but here and there white-gold tendrils curled damply about her face and over her shoulder. Her skin was scrubbed and glowing.

The delightful innocent dressed in virginal white had disappeared, leaving behind a warm, enticing woman. Her unadorned face, her dress, her tousled hair painted, not the image of pristine innocence but a woman to be touched and held. A woman a man wanted to draw down to him, burying his face in the fall of her hair as he loosed the ties of her dress and discovered the sweet secrets beneath.

Secrets he could never know.

With his teeth clenched Patrick forced his attention from the shadowed cleft of her breasts. Looking past her, he expected to find Conroy a step behind. Anger that hovered ever near the surface flared hot and irrational. Conroy should've been there. But, he thought in disgust, what did the photographer know of protecting Jordana?

"Where's your friend?" His voice was a low snarl. "The one who races you up and down a meadow, within inches of a lake." A lake she couldn't see.

"Philip was only doing his job," Jordana defended.

"His job. Your life." If he hadn't been so angry, Patrick would've marveled at her trust. He'd never had that sort of trust, except with Rafe.

"Philip has been my friend for most of my life. He wouldn't hurt me."

"So, where is your friend now?" The last face he wanted to see was Conroy's, yet he was angry that the photographer wasn't here. As he was angry with Randy for being so implacable. With Jordana for being as desirable as ever, and at himself for still wanting her.

Patrick wondered why he was still here. Once he'd seen Jordana safely home from the meadow, why had he lingered? Leaving a woman behind had always been easy. The most intense affair could be ended with a word and a gift. Walking away from a woman he'd met only twice, with whom he'd shared no more than a kiss, should be simple. So why hadn't he walked? Why wasn't he walking now?

Needless questions, and Patrick had little patience with needless questions. He hadn't walked because of two encounters that should've been casual but were not. The first disrupted his life, the second nearly cost hers.

But more than that, he hadn't walked because of the woman. Jordana. He'd wanted her before he knew she was blind. He wanted her now.

The memory that his clumsy arrogance had sent her fleeing from him, and into danger, only served to inflame him. A realist as a rule, in a rare aberration he focused his wrath and guilt on Conroy. "After weeks of standing firm against all my probing, your good friend folded like straw, leaving you to my tender mercies. Where is your good knight?" Patrick fairly spit the sarcasm. "Having trouble facing you?"

"He has nothing to face. I'm here and I'm safe."

Patrick stifled a bitter laugh, wondering if she really believed her own words. Safe? After the kiss in the meadow? Not even the most innocent person could be that naive.

How innocent was she? For the cost of a magazine, any man could buy the replica and lose himself in the enchantment of her golden promise. But what man had turned her promises to reality and lost himself in the real woman? How many? he wondered, and jealousy reared its ugly head.

Patrick had little defenses against it. Before Jordana nothing could have been more foreign to his nature. Now it was a living thing, hidden, waiting to poison his thoughts like an adder. Before Jordana no woman had mattered enough that the touch of another man could anger him.

No one would again, not even Jordana. Not after today, Patrick thought, his face grim as he watched her move across the kitchen. Her step was long, confident, without any hint of hesitation, and he could almost believe that none of what had happened before was real. That she could see.

But he was grasping at straws. Jordana was blind, and like the desire he tried to deny, nothing had changed.

Just short of the counter she stopped. "You're annoyed with Philip. You think he's failed me, but he hasn't. He would be here now, he wanted to be, but I asked him not to." Before Patrick could form a biting reply, Jordana turned toward the woman who watched them like a mother tiger hovering protectively over her cub.

"Randy?" As with Philip in the meadow, Jordana extended her hand, waiting until Randy's closed over it. "Would you leave us? Mr. McCallum and I have something to settle. We shouldn't be long."

Randy folded Jordana's hand in both of hers, searching her friend's calm face. "Are you sure this is what you want?"

"I'm sure."

Randy held Jordana's hand a moment longer, then, with a look of warning for Patrick, she left them. Her footsteps faded, leaving a hush. Patrick wanted Jordana to break the silence, but knew she would not. The first move was his.

She was so close he could catch a hint of the scent she wore. Sunlight and flowers and Jordana. The three were inseparable, and from this day they would always be. "After the travesty in the meadow you have every right to hate me."

"What happened in the meadow was as much my fault as it was yours. I can't hate you for that."

It was hardly the truth, but Patrick did not argue. "Are you afraid of me, Jordana?"

"No." Then, shaking her head, denying her own words, she said, "Yes, you frighten me sometimes. But not now."

Touching his arm, letting her hand rest at his elbow, she smiled a little wistfully. "Come sit with me in the garden. Randy says this is the loveliest time of day."

With her hand still on his arm Patrick went with her and sat by her at a poolside table. He escorted but did not guide, for Jordana needed none.

When she faced him across the table, he had the eerie feeling that her blind eyes saw beyond the veneer to the real Patrick he kept hidden from the world. "How much can you see?" His voice was a tactless, demanding rasp in the serenity of the garden.

"Light, dark. Vague shapes when conditions are right." She was so emotionless she might have been discussing the weather.

"Are conditions right now? Do you see me?"

"No, Patrick," she said almost gently, as if the denial would hurt him. "Other senses tell me what blindness can't. You're sitting down. Your voice is level with me. If you were standing, it would come from much higher." Jordana allowed herself a small chuckle. "Common sense says you're sitting across from me because I heard the scrape of your chair over the stone, and because there's nowhere else to sit at this end of the pool."

"That day in the restaurant, I could've sworn..."

"You were a voice. I couldn't see you. I never will."

He remembered her hand on Conroy's arm, walking with him through the cluster of tiny tables. Regal, calm, guided by trust. Graceful fingers sliding over the contours of the chair, discretely discovering, orienting. An empty glass held with infinite patience, once filled, placed precisely by Jordana. Her surprise at the approach of a stranger. The flash of confusion, wondering, but uncertain if she knew him.

Acts and reactions that had become instinct. So ingrained they served as well with the unexpected. Habits of long standing. Patrick realized he was gripping the edge of the table and willed himself to relax. "How long have you been blind?"

"All my life."

He drew a sharp breath. Somehow he wasn't quite prepared for her answer. He expected years, but not forever. It hadn't occurred to him that she had never seen a sunset, or a flower, or a morning like those he loved in Scotland. He hadn't realized that she had no idea how beautiful she was.

The scent of flowers drifted on a summer breeze. The sun was warm on his skin. Deep in the garden the mockingbird sang, but Patrick did not hear.

"How?" His question rang hollowly between them. Perhaps it was cruelly blunt, but he had to know.

If the bluntness or the cruelty concerned her, Jordana did not show it. Instead, she kept her face toward him, her gaze steady. "I was born prematurely. There was an accident in an incubator. They weren't uncommon twenty-eight years ago."

"Surely your family tried to do something, find some way, some remedy. Medicine is always changing. There are new cures and new procedures being developed every day."

"They tried. Up until the day my father died, he was trying. I was nine. Within the next year my grandmother had put a stop to the searching. Irreversible damage, she said, was simply that, irreversible.

"She was right in that at least." Something flickered in her face, something Patrick had never seen. It was there and gone too rapidly to interpret.

"Your grandmother resented your blindness, didn't she?" He ventured the guess that would explain the look he'd seen. "She resented you for not being perfect."

"It was the second strike against me." Her smile was bleak, and Patrick discovered that even sightless eyes could be sad. But again it was only a fleeting impression, one she didn't dwell on. In a matter-of-fact fashion she continued. "The first thing was that I wasn't male. Someone who could perpetuate the Daniel name. Now that my mother has remarried and lives in Switzerland, there are only two of us, Grandmother Emma, and me. A bitter old woman, and a blind one. The last of the Daniel dynasty."

"You have no contact with your grandmother?"

"She has refused to see me since I was eighteen."

"What happened when you were eighteen, Jordana? What could an eighteen-year-old do that was so terrible in the eyes of Emma Daniel that she couldn't forgive in ten years?"

"My grandmother is a very old-fashioned and proper Southern lady. Correct, proud, inordinately concerned with family and upholding its reputation. She was a throwback to an era when a child like me was kept hidden. A source of shame one never admitted. Without my father my mother was no match for her and neither was I. Until I was eighteen and I rebelled. Then her little world knew her secret. One of her own was defective.

"She was afraid her friends would pity her for having a grandchild like me. The one thing we have in common is that we both abhor pity. She chose to deny, and I to impugn. Grandmother, granddaughter, different perspectives, different methods, estranged because of them."

Patrick was not a compassionate man. He was too hard for compassion. Yet as Jordana sat in the slanting light of the afternoon sun, speaking of shame and horror, he wanted to take her in his arms, telling her it was not she who was a horror and a shame, but the proud, rigid Emma Daniel.

The feeling was too new and the words beyond him. The moment passed and it was too late. In its aftermath he sat quietly, wondering why Jordana, who had been elusive and aloof for weeks, had chosen to tell such a private and painful story to a virtual stranger. Every instinct that made him the shrewd and successful magnate said this was an extraordinary, perhaps singular, happening. Again he wondered why.

"Why?"

For an unsettling instant Patrick thought she had read his mind. But a look at her closed expression, and he knew she was simply thinking aloud. He wouldn't push. When she was ready, she would explain. Patience, like compassion, was never his nature, but he would wait.

As if she were weary of the tension, Jordana touched her temple with her fingertips, pressing lightly at the vein that pulsed beneath her skin. Then slowly she slid her hand through her hair, combing her fingers through it, adding to the irresistible dishevelment.

To the world she was mysterious, elusive, a dream. Here in her garden she was flesh and blood, with the troubles and the needs of a real woman. If the world were not already at her feet, it would be, if it saw this Jordana.

"I have questions, Patrick." A rare frown creased her brow. She shook her head, searching for a beginning. "I know so much about you. When you began to ask your own questions about me, and persisted against the odds, Randy made it a point to find out all she could about you. I know of your phenomenal success in business, and as an athlete, and with women. Tabloids and respectable papers alike keep tabs on your ever-changing liaisons.

"I know of your lands in Scotland, of your father and how close you were. Only your mother is a shadowy figure. There's nothing about her. As if she never existed.

"I know that there's a private Patrick who's more than the newspapers portray. Just as there's a private Jordana who has little in common with the Jordana who appears on the magazine covers and advertisements. Truth and fantasy, and no common ground."

Jordana heard her own bitterness. It had not been there for years, but now it was unmistakable. It had to do with Patrick McCallum.

"Ask your questions, Jordana." After pursuing her for weeks and bursting unannounced and uninvited into her life, he owed her that much. Perhaps it was this that had kept him here far longer than he intended, a need to make right the incident in the meadow. That done, he would make his exit with as much grace as he could muster. "I promise you, I'll try to answer any question you wish."

Patrick didn't stop to think that these were concessions he wouldn't have made twenty-four hours ago. Nor that he would've made them to no one but Jordana.

"My questions are simple. They begin with why."

"Then ask me the whys, if they will ease your mind." If Patrick had heard the gentleness in his voice, he would have been astonished, but he didn't hear, for all his thoughts were on the troubled woman before him.

"The truth?" Everything she had learned about this man indicated that he was brutally honest. But would he be with her? "The truth, no matter if it hurts?"

"Yes."

"Then we'll begin with two. Why are you here? Now that you are, after weeks of searching, why are you leaving?"

"You know why I came. You know why I'm leaving. Why I have to leave." Randy, with her tough talk and street smarts, could take lessons in going for the jugular from this lady.

Jordana heard the surge of anger in him, sensed the uncommon agitation. "You haven't answered me, Patrick."

"Dammit, Jordana! What do you want me to say?"

"You approached me in the restaurant...."

"Let's not mince words. I came on to you."

"All right." Jordana inclined her head. "You came on to me. Why?"

"Why? Good God! Why does a man come on to a woman? Because he wants her."

"Why? Why did you want me? How could one look be enough? You didn't know me or anything about me."

"You're a beautiful woman. You have no idea how beautiful. I was tired, bored. My world was ugly and jaded, and it was my fault. Too much fast living with no real values. You were sunlight in darkness. Sunlight that I wanted." He promised honesty, honesty she would have. "You were what I needed. When you looked at me as if I didn't exist, you became more than a need. You became an obsession."

"So you searched for me, leaving no avenue unexplored, but with no success."

"Until Rafe Courtenay, my CEO, caught a rumor that proved true. He called in a favor and traced you through Richard Chassen, the sponsor of the Summer Girl project. I was so fascinated by you that I came from Scotland, intending this time to have you."

"By having me you mean sleep with me?"

"Yes. Sleep with you, find solace for an ache that hasn't gone away since the moment I saw you. An ache that no other woman can ease." The truth. "Because I haven't

wanted any woman but you since I saw you. *That's* obsession, and I was obsessed.''

Jordana heard the past tense. ''It ended with a kiss and
the discovery that your perfect woman wasn't quite so
perfect. You bought the fantasy, and reality destroyed it.''

Emma Daniel had dealt with Jordana's blindness by
hiding her away. Patrick asked himself if running was any
better. The answer was ugly. With a muffled groan and
gritted teeth he asked, ''What would you have me do,
Jordana?''

''Something happened in the meadow when you kissed
me. It shocked you and frightened me, because it was new
to both of us. See it through. Give us time to discover what
it was.''

''You don't know what you're asking.''

''I'll take my chances.''

He wanted to shake her, make her listen to reason. ''I'm
trouble, and you have enough trouble in your life.''

''I can deal with trouble. Better than with pity.''

''Pity?'' It hadn't occurred to him to pity her. He regretted that she'd lived twenty-eight years without her
sight. Regretted all the beautiful things she had never seen.
But regret wasn't pity. ''God help me, I have no idea what
I feel or why, but it isn't pity.''

Jordana knew a part of it was fear. She'd encountered
it many times. The self-conscious malaise. The discomfort. The dread of making a mistake. The raised voice as
if she were deaf. The hovering. The careful handling as if
she would break. Fear and revulsion because she was different. As hateful as pity.

''Then shouldn't we explore it to discover what it is and
resolve it? Mustn't we, for your sake as well as mine?'' He
had come like a conquerer to take the spoils of his victory.
If she succeeded, when he left he would understand her, as

well. His stare was on her. She felt the weight of it and was glad for once that she couldn't see. This was one of the rare times when the darkness of her world made it easier to say what she must. "By your own admission there's been no woman in your recent life. A veritable drought for the virile Patrick McCallum."

"Are you volunteering?"

"Perhaps. But not if you're in Scotland."

He had never been bested by a woman, but he was wise enough to recognize defeat and strong enough to admit it. "I'll be here, Jordana, not in Scotland." He sighed heavily. "God help me, I hope this isn't a mistake."

"It's too late to worry about mistakes, Patrick. It was too late from the first."

"I suppose it was." He studied her face with the hint of fatigue shadowing it. "I should leave. You're tired. It's been . . . an unusual day, for both of us."

Sliding back his chair, he stood. The coolness within his shadow fell over her as he blocked out sun. She waited for him to speak, to set their course.

"Randy asked me to dinner. Would you thank her for me and tell her another time?" He touched her face, tracing the soft contour of her cheek with the pad of his thumb. He wanted to kiss her but didn't dare. "I have some things to sort out in my mind."

Jordana barely resisted turning her lips into his palm and was shocked at the madness of it. He was a stranger, formidable and arrogant, and she had decided to teach him a lesson. But with a touch, her plan had gone awry. Patrick McCallum was dangerous—very dangerous—and she must never forget.

"I think . . ." Her mouth was dry, her throat tight as her heart threatened to leap from her chest. "I think we both have some things to sort out."

He took a step back, and sunlight washed over her. "Tomorrow?"

She lifted her face toward his voice. This was what she wanted. "Yes. Tomorrow."

Four

———

A stealthy footstep ruffled the quiet. A light step, nearly lost in the whisper of the breeze. Though she only drowsed, Jordana pretended sleep, listening for another step and then another. With a shriek a compact body was on her, wiggling, giggling, scattering kisses over her face.

"I got you!" Cassie crowed with the delight of a mischievous child. "You didn't hear me coming!"

"Cass!" Jordana feigned surprise as she swung her long bare legs over the chaise lounge. "Where on earth did you come from?" Grasping the child before she could dance away, Jordana dragged her squealing and laughing into her arms, kissing the spot that never failed to bring giggles. "You were so quiet you must have dropped from the sky."

"No." Cassie grinned, ready for the game they played.

"You floated by on a big balloon. A red one, as red as my bikini, but with yellow elephants painted on the side."

The child clapped her hands, waiting for the next outrageous guess.

"It was a real elephant. He caught you up in his purple trunk and *voilà!* Here you are. No!" Jordana paused as if just struck by an idea. "No, not a purple elephant! A green one."

"No, silly." Cassie doubled over in giggles and slid bonelessly from Jordana's embrace to the stone that bordered the pool. "It was a van that was green. I did draw an elephant at camp, though. Mom stuck him on the refrigerator door. Would you like me to tell you about him?"

Jordana chuckled. The elephant had been more than a lucky guess. Cassie was fascinated with them. She had been since she was a baby. Even at nine, when she was ill or distressed she still dragged out Funny Fanny, the tattered elephant she'd slept with as a baby. Funny Fanny, Jordana's first gift to Randy's child.

"I'd like very much to hear about your elephant." With a beckoning finger Jordana made room for the child on her lounge. "Come sit with me and tell me all about him." With Cassie sheltered comfortably beneath her arm, she launched again into nonsense. "How long is his trunk? Longer than his tail? How many legs does he have? Are they all green and are his toenails shocking pink?"

"No, silly." Cassie's favorite phrase of late. "Humphrey's a real elephant and he's gray."

"Gray!" Jordana said in mock distress with her own obtuseness. "Ah! Of course, he's gray. The color the world's best-dressed Humphreys are wearing. But—" she leaned closer to whisper "—I do hope his toenails are pink."

Cassie promptly burst into giggles again.

In the study off the kitchen, Randy put aside the menus for the coming week, drawn by the sound to the window overlooking the pool. The frown that had lingered over her features all day vanished as she watched her friend and daughter teasing as if they were of an age.

"I swear—" Randy shook her head "—when they start their foolishness I don't know which giggles the most."

She scoffed, but gently, for it was the sound she'd waited for. The time when Cassie came home from day camp and drew Jordana from her puzzling mood.

Last evening, after Patrick had left, and then Philip, Randy expected questions and explanations, even accusations. But Jordana had been quiet . . . too quiet. Through dinner she was distracted, abruptly excusing herself, claiming fatigue. Yet, in the night, Randy heard her wandering the house.

This morning, immediately after the breakfast she barely touched, Jordana had locked herself in her small studio to work. Creating music, stories and songs meant for children was her true vocation. The work she loved.

Jordana had never studied the piano or the guitar, yet she played and composed like a professional. When she was satisfied with lyric and melody, she would play and sing into a recorder. The recording was then scored by an expert in such matters. Later it would be produced and distributed by the small company formed by Jordana years ago. The company, simply called Soar, was discreet and nonprofit. Meant only to offer inspiration to children. Children who were blind or deaf, who suffered from learning disorders, birth defects or disease. And the normal child who simply needed encouragement.

In Randy's judgment Jordana was a remarkable woman, concerned, generous and multitalented. Jordana's generosity did not extend to herself or her talents. Once in the early days of their friendship, in answer to Randy's praise, a hidden bitterness had surfaced in the term *idiot savant.* Randy's answering fury had been awesome. With every expletive and invective she'd ever known, and inventing others along the way, she'd cursed, not Jordana, but Emma Daniel. The ugly label was exactly the sort the cruel and very proper old witch would use to mark a hurting child. When her rage was exhausted, if not ended, Randy had finished with the promise that she would cut Emma's heart out before she would let her near Cassie.

The term, never spoken before, was never spoken again.

Randy rarely thought about that ugly day, for the bitterness that prompted it was rare. Jordana had come to terms with her problems and put regrets aside. From that day forward she became too eager to learn and too happy with the world to let the stupidity of others hamper her.

At least she had until recently. The exuberance of the eighteen-year-old just discovering a life she'd been denied by a mean-spirited old woman had gradually dimmed. It was in part the natural toll of maturing, and in part something darker and disturbing.

Randy had watched the sobering, hating it but powerless to stop it. Then Patrick McCallum had burst into the ever-shrinking circle of Jordana's life. Stubborn, determined, by his own admission cocky and roughshod. He was intrigued by the mystery, provoked by her indifference and fevered with the need to possess her. He could be disaster or godsend.

Yesterday Randy had gambled on the latter. Today she questioned her own sanity. With Cassie at day camp and Jordana locked away in the studio, she had gone about her day in a state of worry. As she listened to chord after chord, each more dissonant and distracted, it was painfully obvious Jordana's music was not going well.

Jordana was troubled, and Randy did not question that its source was Patrick McCallum. Which meant the blame rested squarely on her head.

With uncommon restraint she'd suffered the long day, waiting for an opening, a chance to help if she could. Opportunity never came. Lunch was as quiet as dinner, her friend as unapproachable. Then Jordana had dressed in her swimsuit and settled in at her favorite spot by the pool, and Randy's hopes had risen. Now, listening and watching the special joy shared with a child, there was more than hope.

"I know exactly what this party needs." Spinning on her heels, she went to the kitchen. Loading a tray with the newest batch of chocolate-chip cookies, a pitcher of lemonade and three paper cups, she headed for the pool.

"Cookies!" Cassie crowed at the sight of the tray.

"A peace offering," Randy murmured as she set the tray on the table by Jordana and took the seat across from her.

"Have you been fighting with someone, Mom?"

"No, darling, I just made a mistake."

"Oh." Cassie immediately lost interest as she grabbed a second cookie. "Can I swim awhile before dinner, Mom?"

"Sure."

"Great!" Cassie never walked when she could run, and she didn't now.

Randy watched as she disappeared into the house, then turned to Jordana. "I'm sorry."

Jordana was completely mystified. "For what?"

"For yesterday. For sending Patrick to the meadow. I know you've been upset with me all day."

"I'm not angry with you, Randy. It hadn't occurred to me to blame you. Why should I?"

"I shouldn't have sent him to the meadow."

"You couldn't have stopped him."

"But I told him exactly where you were."

"He would have found us. You only speeded him along by a matter of a few minutes." With her tone as much as her words, Jordana declared Randy guiltless. "Is there lemonade?"

"Isn't there always?" Randy's chuckle was more relief than humor.

After lemonade was placed in her hand, Jordana sipped it, then held the icy cup between her palms, savoring its coolness against her warm skin. "I was puzzled by what I overheard in the kitchen. You seemed to think it was important that he become a part of my life. Why, Randy?"

"We've always been honest with each other." Randy hesitated, questioning the wisdom of it now.

"We have. Your honesty and your opinions have played a major part in my adult life."

"Then I don't suppose now's the time to change it." Saying it was easier than believing it, but, gathering her thoughts and her resolve, Randy launched into an explanation. "Your impression was right. I did want Patrick to stay in your life. You need someone. Someone brazen and irreverent. Someone who will get you back into life. Since you've been modeling for Philip..." Randy shook her head, unsure how to continue.

"With the celebrity, I've moved into a shell," Jordana supplied.

"And you mustn't. You have too much to offer to shut yourself away."

"To offer a man, you mean."

"Only a man who can appreciate you."

"You think Patrick is that man?"

"Patrick, or a man like him. Someone strong because, withdrawing or not, you're a strong woman. You've had to be. A weak man could never understand you. Philip, for example. He knows your history, he was with you for part of it when his father was your grandmother's gardener. He should understand, yet he only sees a pretty face he can put to selfish use. He has no concept of your faith and spirit. He could never in a lifetime of trying match your strength."

"So you've chosen Patrick for me."

"Patrick chose himself for you."

Jordana found an empty space by the tray and set the cup down. "Until he discovered I can't see."

"So he is leaving." Randy sagged in disappointment. Some men only happened once in a lifetime. There wouldn't be another Patrick. Perhaps it would've come to nothing, but deep in her heart Randy was certain there was more to his interest than sex. She was too sensible to believe in love at first sight. But if not at first sight, it had to start somewhere. Patrick's single-minded interest was certainly a start.

"Patrick isn't leaving. And I think I've made the biggest mistake of my life."

"Mistake?" Randy was both glad and alarmed.

"I was angry and irritated and exasperated." Jordana shrugged and sighed, leaving it to Randy's imagination. "You know I hate it when people act as if I'm made of glass."

"So? What have you done, Jordana?"

"What do we really know about Patrick, except that he rises to a challenge? I've been a challenge from the first." Jordana laughed humorlessly. "It was a part of my mystique."

"Finding you was a challenge." Randy was on track with Jordana and knew where she was headed. "He isn't leaving because you offered another challenge, dared him to stay."

"Bingo! A part of me wants to teach him a lesson, another part simply wants him to stay."

"So where's the mistake?"

Jordana drew her legs up, wrapped her arms about them and propped her chin on her knees. "He kissed me."

"And?"

"And it was scary."

"There are two ways to be scared. One's nice and exciting. The other's mean and nasty. Patrick McCallum may be a conceited, overbearing son of a Scot and he may need a notch or two taken out of his ego, but mean? I'd bet the man doesn't really have a mean bone in his body." Randy tensed, her eyes glittered. "But if I thought so I'd..."

"Randy, no." Jordana stopped her in midsentence. "He wasn't exactly gentle, but he didn't hurt me. I don't think he would ever hurt me physically."

"Then what?"

"It scared me because I liked it. I wanted him to kiss me again. I've never felt anything like it." Her voice was low, muffled against her knee. "It was like something warm and delicious curling through me, gathering intensity until I couldn't think or breathe. Then it was over." She stopped, her eyes closed, reliving the kiss. "Even when he wasn't touching me, I was still trembling inside."

"Honey, that's what it's like to kiss a man."

"I've been kissed before."

"Not by Patrick."

"No." Her voice dropped another level, becoming only a breath. "Not by Patrick."

"You're intelligent, Jordana, intelligent enough to know that if he stays in your life, you'll have choices to make. You're a beautiful and desirable woman. He's a virile man and he wants you. That's your choice. Perhaps the most important you will ever make. Do you want him?"

"I don't know."

"You'll know. When the time comes, you'll know." Randy stroked the shining fall of Jordana's hair, her fingers an ebony comb sliding through liquid pearls. "Just be careful."

Jordana's laugh was humorless. "It's a little late to be careful, isn't it?"

"It's never too late to be careful." Randy patted her shoulder, wondering if there was a special hell for people who threw kittens in the paths of lions and blithely told them to be careful. But could this kitten tame the lion? Stranger things had happened. "When will you be seeing him again?"

"He said today, but he also said he had some things to sort out in his mind."

"I imagine he does," Randy muttered. Then, seeing the forlorn look on Jordana's face, she said cheerfully, "I have an idea. Let's have a party tonight."

"Why would we have a party?"

"We need a reason? How about because it's Friday? Or because it isn't my birthday? Or because there's an elephant named Humphrey on the refrigerator?"

Jordana was smiling now. "Let's celebrate Humphrey."

"Humphrey it is! And Humphrey rates a special dress. You haven't worn the blue in a while, and I've a slinky number that could stand some dusting off. I could even whip up a special dessert. Since Cass can stay up later tonight, let's make it a sophisticated hour. At eight, by the pool?"

"Eight it is."

Randy stood, brushing at her slacks. "Cassie must be having trouble finding her suit. "I'd better check."

Jordana listened to the patter of her steps, hard on the stone, softer over the grass, then quiet. She was alone in the garden with her thoughts of Patrick.

He hadn't intended this. He knew it was crazy. Rafe would second that opinion without hesitation. Patrick knew that if he'd had any sense at all he'd have been on the jet to Scotland by the time the sun was rising.

He had promised *her* tomorrow. And tomorrow had come.

Shifting in the seat, he cursed when his knee hit the gear. At six-five he was too tall for Rafe's roadster, but discomfort was not the true reason for his ill humor. "Fool!" he muttered. What he'd learned of Jordana warned that he was the last person she needed in her life.

What he'd learned—so much, yet so little. Once he had a name, the volume of information that followed was astounding. Most of it about the prominent Daniel family and its history. Little about Jordana, yet enough to read an ugly story between the lines. Those who knew the Daniels before Henry's death remembered a child. Some recalled a hint of scandal, others alluded to tragedy connected to Henry Daniel's little girl. Since they'd neither seen nor heard of her in years, most assumed she had died, as well. Not one made the connection between the Daniel family and the beautiful woman who graced the covers of so many magazines.

Emma Daniel had succeeded in hiding the child far better than he expected. The child who had become an intriguing woman. The woman who was drawing him into her web.

"Fool." He spit the accusation even as he turned the car into the curving drive that would lead to Jordana.

As he stepped to the drive, pocketing the key, the only light he saw was a dim glow at the back of the house. He'd already discovered that she loved the garden and the sunlight. Perhaps it applied to twilight, as well. Except, he reminded himself with a jolt, she couldn't see the twilight. Dammit, he was in over his head. An unfamiliar feeling. One he hated.

Turn around, McCallum, the voice of reason whispered as he took the path to the garden. Turn around, get in the car and drive away. The voice was more urgent; he knew he should heed it. Instead, he kept walking. As he turned the corner, he was met by laughter and flickering candlelight.

There were three of them, seated at a table laden with the remnants of a meal. Jordana wore the blue gown he would never forget, Randy, white, and the child who was obviously Randy's daughter, bright pink. From their mood and dress, it was a celebration.

He stepped onto the terrace that circled the pool and saw Jordana tense. It was disconcerting, but of course she would sense his presence before the others.

"Patrick." She turned to him. His step, already familiar, set her heart racing.

"Intruding has become my habit."

"Mr. McCallum." Randy was rising to meet him. "We were just finishing, but if you'd like something?"

"Thanks, no. This looks like a party."

"We're celebrating Humphrey," the child piped in.

"My daughter, Cassie," Randy offered as explanation.

"Hi, Cassie. I'm Patrick, but who's Humphrey?"

"He's an elephant who lives on the refrigerator." The child was eager to explain.

"An elephant that lives in the refrigerator?"

"No, silly, not in it. He'd be too big."

"I imagine he would be."

"I drew him at day camp and we decided to celebrate."

"Ah, I see." Patrick grinned. He had little experience with children, but he suspected this one was unlike most children.

"Cassie, it's after eight. If we're going to see the video before your bedtime, we'd better get started. Mr. McCallum." Randy nodded at him then looked to Jordana. "Jordana?"

"I'll be in shortly, Randy." Until now, beyond calling his name, Jordana hadn't spoken. She'd been content to listen to the teasing timbre of his voice, matching it with what Randy had told her of his looks.

He was tall, but she'd discovered that for herself, from the great distance his voice rose above her and when he'd bent to kiss her. His body was massive but trim. That, too, she knew by the feel of him against her. His hair was dark auburn. Randy likened it to the leaves of late fall, saying it curled over his collar. His skin was like pale copper, and his eyes shone in contrast like brilliant sapphires. Colors Jordana could only imagine. There were scars, Randy said. One at his brow, the other at his lip. Had he been hurt in the rough Highland games he was so fond of? Jordana was left to imagine and conjecture.

He wasn't a handsome man, but given his size and coloring, he was certainly the most striking around. When he walked into a room, Randy assured her, there wasn't a woman who was not instantly aware.

As Jordana was aware, with his first step on the terrace. Just as she was aware that he was watching her now. Because she could think of nothing wise or witty, she fell back on stilted courtesies. "Hello. How was your day?"

"A good one." His day was a disaster, but he didn't intend she would ever know he'd spent it barking unneces-

sary orders and snapping at people who didn't deserve it.
Even Rafe had looked at him with something akin to pity,
suggesting he either get the woman out of his system or go
home to Scotland. Then the chaos Patrick created could be
undone by cooler heads.

Rafe's pity had set his hackles rising. He remembered
how Jordana hated pity. Such was his day, a mass of con-
voluted circles, all leading to Jordana.

Clasping her glass, she stroked its fluted lines. "I wasn't
sure you would come."

"Neither was I."

"Why did you?"

"I wish I knew." But he did know why... he wanted to
see her again, as she was now. Calm, reserved, with only
the pulse fluttering at her temple to prove the calm a lie.

"Would you like to sit down?"

"No." The word was bitten off more brusquely than he
intended. "No," he repeated more civilly. "The drive from
Atlanta was long. I need to stretch my legs."

"Would you like to walk in the garden? It's lovely when
the moon is first rising."

"I'd like that." He watched as she rose, saw the blue
fabric straining over her breasts and the skirt sway about
her hips. When she was standing, he knew the next move
was his. "How do we do this?" His question was a low
growl, an arrogant man's frustration. "You'll have to help
me."

"There's no trick to it. I take your arm, like this." Sliding her arm through his, she laid her hand over his wrist.
She smiled up at him, then, for the first time. An enchanting smile that played havoc with his heart.

Jordana's garden was a profusion of flowers and vines,
clustered along meandering walks. The air was redolent
with their scent, and she knew them all. At a scraggly,

fragrant plant she stopped, bending to pluck a long stem. "For Cassie," she explained and reached for him again. "She loves four-o'clocks."

From the moment her hand left his arm he'd wondered what it was like to cut oneself off from everything and venture into the dark. It must take a great deal of courage. Every day would take courage. And trust, in herself, in her abilities, in those about her. When her hand was sliding over his arm once more, he felt that trust and was shockingly humbled by it. "What..." He heard the rawness and, clearing his throat, tried again. "What are four-o'clocks?"

Jordana laughed, a sound as silvery as the rising moon. "I suppose it sounds like a ridiculous name, but they come by it honestly. Well, almost honestly. The flowers only open in the late afternoon. I've never checked the time to be certain it's actually four o'clock, but it's close enough. Cassie likes to watch them open and close. They aren't a pretty plant, but the fragrance is wonderful."

"They look like weeds."

"Some people would agree. The gardener grumbled the whole time he was planting them. He made dire predictions that they would take the garden, and they have, this corner at least. But the scent is worth it." She matched her pace to his. "What are the flowers like in Scotland?"

Patrick said the one thing he knew. "They're pretty."

"That's it?"

"That's all I know."

"Then tell me about the Scotland you do know."

As they strolled deeper among the flowers, Patrick told her of his Scotland, searching for words that would make her understand. He was keenly aware of the sway of her body, the brush of her breast, as she hugged his arm closer, listening raptly to every word.

"It must be wonderful," she said when he finished. "There are so many beautiful places."

He heard the wistful note. "Have you traveled?"

"Very little. Randy and I spent four years in school in Switzerland. But other than Atlanta and here, very little else. I know there are wonderful places with strange and exotic names or simple names. Cassie's a whiz at geography and at the moment she's into videos. I sit in sometimes, listening."

"Geography and elephants? An unusual combination."

"Cassie's an unusual child."

The entire household was unusual. A beautiful Southern woman who could have been the prototype for the fabled California girl, the forgotten grandchild of one of the South's wealthiest men. A mystery woman who modeled, but hated the limelight. Who was blind and wanted to see the world.

An elegant black woman with the manner of a grand lady who spoke the language of the streets like a pro. Who was as familiar with a switchblade as a vegetable peeler. Who hovered over her charge like a mother hen with a wounded chick.

A gifted child, whose father was never mentioned.

For every question answered, there were dozens more. If he weren't already fascinated, he would be now. His time in America promised to be interesting, the woman at his side most of all. "Where would you like to go? What would you like to..." He caught himself, disturbed with his choice of words.

"What would I like to see?" Jordana smiled. "It's a perfectly good word, Patrick. Don't be uneasy when you use it. Don't be uneasy with any words."

"I won't, not again." She abhorred pity and pretentious concern, but hated the distress she caused as much. She was a courageous woman, but he wondered if he had any concept of the expense of her courage. Patrick, the first to admit little compassion, wanted to hold her, lending his strength to hers. Instead, he drew her closer and resumed their walk. "So tell me, what would you like to see?"

"Many places. The Grand Canyon, the Rockies, the Blue Ridge, Yosemite, Australia, Scotland."

"Scotland?"

"You make it sound wonderful."

"Perhaps someday you can go there."

"I don't think so."

Patrick heard the yearning and hoped one day she could have what she wanted, just as he was about to take what he wanted. What he'd wanted since the moment he'd seen her sitting with the flickering light of the candle kissing her face.

Slowing his pace, he stopped, turning her to him. He'd wanted this, but hadn't planned it. Just as he hadn't planned being here. He was discovering that where Jordana was concerned, plans meant nothing. He touched her face, stroking her cheek with the back of his hand. "I know you don't like sudden or unexpected moves, so I'm warning you. I'm going to kiss you, Jordana. Now."

His hands slid from her face into her hair, his fingers curling through it, keeping her close as his mouth descended to hers.

She turned to meet him, her body brushing his, igniting banked fires. Her lips were warm and sweet, parting slowly beneath his. It was an innocent, unpracticed kiss, ended quickly, but it rocked him. When he lifted his head and drew her against him, he wondered what in heaven's name she did to him.

Jordana was grateful that he held her. Grateful for his strength, for hers had flown. She was unsteady as they turned in silent consent and began the walk back through the garden.

"I told myself I wouldn't do that," Patrick said into the gathering darkness.

"I promised myself the same." Her fingers grasped his shirt. "We're strangers. How can it be like this?"

"The answer to the whole madness has eluded me for weeks."

The grimness was back in his voice, and with it a ruthless resolve that swept over her like ice. Patrick was a man from another world, who'd had many women in his life. This was hardly special to him. Perhaps it was the way of all his conquests. A riddle fascinated until it was solved. An itch irritated until it was scratched.

Jordana's stomach churned, and her throat burned. She wanted to pull away from him, but she was lost. As they'd wandered, she hadn't kept track; she had no idea where they were.

"Will you be working tomorrow?"

"Working?" His question took her by surprise.

"With Conroy."

"Philip left before dinner last night," she answered absently, her mind too chaotic to think of Philip. "He'll be gone a week."

Patrick found dour satisfaction in the photographer's absence. He wouldn't be touching her. "I have some things to do tomorrow, some fences to mend, but I'll be back."

"No." She felt the stone of the terrace under her feet and drew back, feeling safe from him, from herself, only when his hand fell away. "You were right yesterday, you should go."

"Back to Scotland?"

"To anywhere, just not here."

"You didn't think that when you kissed me. You did kiss me, Jordana, and you wanted me as much as I want you."

"It was a mistake. I don't want to make a worse one."

"It's too late. We both knew that yesterday."

"Patrick..."

"Shh." He stopped her with a finger over her lips, then let it linger to stroke their trembling softness. "I want to kiss you again, but if I do, I won't leave you, and I have to go. But next time, Jordana, I'm not sure I can." His warning given, he moved away. "Randy's lurking by the door, worrying."

Then, only because he couldn't resist her, he leaned to brush her mouth lightly with a quick kiss.

He still did not touch her, nor hold her as his mouth took hers again.

"No." The word was torn from her even as she was rising to meet him.

His kiss was deliberate, demanding, until her lips softened in the response he wanted, the response she'd tried to deny him. As deliberately as he'd kissed her, he moved away, leaving her wanting more as badly as he.

"Yes," he murmured. Perhaps it was a promise, perhaps a threat; not even he knew as he brushed the back of his hand over her cheek. "Yes, Jordana, and there's nothing either of us can do to stop it."

His smile was a slash across his grim face as he left her swaying like the flowers in her garden.

Five

Patrick looked up from the brief he was reading, his concentration broken by the strum of Jordana's guitar. With Cassie at her side, she sat on the floor, weaving a marvelous combination of story and song. Seduced by the melody and by Jordana, he abandoned the pretense of work.

He had come back to her, time and again in the three weeks since the celebration of Humphrey. In those weeks he hadn't held her or kissed her. Hostage to his own needs, he was in the middle of nowhere, biding his time when he should be in London. Matters there clamored for his attention. When he did go, his next stop would be Scotland. Then it would be months before he returned to America.

London needed him. He needed Scotland. But first there was Jordana.

He was as amazed as Rafe that he didn't just cut his losses and go. He'd never in his life been this patient with a woman. Never needed or wanted to mix romance with sex. Affairs began for whatever reason, a whim, a passing fancy, boredom, opportunity. As they began, they ended. As simply as that. Patrick was well versed in the art of seduction, but a novice at courtship. Yet he was courting Jordana.

A year ago, even half a year, he would've laughed if anyone had predicted he would lose his head over a woman. Any woman, especially one like Jordana.

She was unlike any he'd ever encountered. Her blindness was incontrovertible, but with time and familiarity and a glimmer of understanding, it was no longer a deterrent. He'd grown accustomed to it. Though he'd never stop regretting it, he had accepted it. After a clumsy start he learned to deal with the problems. It was second nature to put things in their expected places; to guide, not lead; to help only when truly needed.

Jordana amazed him, moving through a world that was only a mass of shadows, seeing more clearly than one dependent on sight. An extraordinary woman, but not for him. His head told him so repeatedly. His body did not listen.

His body was not listening now.

Randy was in the kitchen. Philip Conroy had come and gone, but not before the two of them bristled like pit bulls. Patrick contended Conroy was too demanding. Conroy declared he'd known Jordana a lifetime, and big red Scots should just stay out of the way. Jordana, wanting to be finished with work and wrangling, finally intervened, sending Patrick away.

He'd hated leaving her with Conroy. The photographer's hands were constantly on her. It was direction, and Conroy was only a friend, but Patrick liked it not one bit more.

There was no Conroy now, yet he was no less troubled, no less restless. Her music surrounded him, a simple melody that would haunt him when he was not with her. Sprawled at her side, Cassie was entranced by the story, lost in the world of imagination. There was no one to see as he studied Jordana openly, searching for the elusive qualities that kept him here when he should be somewhere else. Could be with someone else.

It wasn't just that she was beautiful. He could name a dozen women as beautiful, any one of whom he could summon with a phone call. No, it wasn't beauty that bound him to Jordana. It was her smile, the way she tilted her head when she listened, the jut of her chin when she was frightened. An aura that surrounded her, something he knew in his heart, but had no word to explain. She was light and color, kindness and warmth. She was honesty and courage. She was sensuality and innocence.

And how many times must he remind himself? Not his type at all.

He should pick up the phone and summon one of those dozen hard-eyed, worldly women who had never been innocent. Who understood the rules he played by. Who would accept rubies and diamonds as their due and walk away unscathed.

Jordana had never played that game. She wouldn't understand when the time came for rubies and diamonds. She wouldn't understand at all. He would hurt her; he hated the thought. But no matter how he tried, he couldn't walk away.

Paper crackled in his hand, and the report he'd been reading was reduced to rubbish. With a silent oath he tossed it aside and bolted to his feet. He was halfway across the room that whispered softly of her scent when he realized she'd stopped playing.

"Patrick, is something wrong?"

She knew. She always knew. She sensed his moods, if not the cause, before he did. A woman so intuitive would be an exquisite lover.

"Patrick?"

He heard the beginning of concern. He dared not look at her. "Just restless, Jordana. Go on with your story. Nothing's wrong. I'm just going out for a walk."

"Cassie and I could go."

"No." For three weeks he'd been circumspect, rarely touching her and then only to guide. Tonight he was incapable of circumspection. "I have some thinking to do."

He didn't wait for an answer. Instead, he stalked through the house toward the kitchen, seeking the peace and darkness of the garden.

"Things getting a little sticky, Mr. McCallum?"

Randy was putting a roast in the oven to cook through the night. Patrick's glare met with a lazy grin. She called him by his surname or his given name as it suited her mood. Mr. McCallum was usually reserved for mocking.

"Who the hell are you and what do you want out of this?" he snarled, stopping short.

"I thought you'd figured that out by now." Her hands were on her hips, her shoulders back. "I'm the lady Jordana picked up off the street, and I want her to be happy."

"You think I'm the key to her happiness?"

"Jury's still out, but I think you're her best shot."

"Jordana needs more than I can give her."

"Nobody's asking you for forever. Just like some lifetimes can be lived in a little while, some happiness can last a lifetime. Cassie's proof of that." She shrugged, grinning again. "Who knows, you might fool yourself and stick. Look at me. Ten years later I'm still with her."

Patrick grinned, too, not pleasantly. "You turn that tough-lady act off and on like a faucet, don't you?"

"Serves its purpose."

"Who are you really? How did you come to Jordana?"

"It's a long story."

"I have until tomorrow. In case you've forgotten, you were the one who decided it was ridiculous to drive back and forth to Atlanta when there were extra bedrooms here. A decision you've lived to regret, Ms. Taylor?"

"Touché." Randy gave a mocking salute, then fell silent, gathering her thoughts. "I suppose where you're concerned I'm ambivalent. I want you to stay, I want you to go. I think you're right for Jordana, I think you're wrong. I think you're what she needs, I think you're the last thing she needs. Ambivalence! That explains my ill humor. Yours needs no explaining.

"You want a story, perhaps it's time you had it." Going to a cabinet, she brought out a bottle of Scotch, poured a generous drink and handed it to him. "You just might need this before it's done."

Seated with her at the table, with Jordana framed like a work of art by the archway leading to the adjoining room, he heard a tale of horror, of narrow-minded hatred and ugly pride. Jordana's version bore only a vague resemblance to Randy's. Even when she should hate, there was a kindness in Jordana.

"That's what her life was like from the time she was nine until she was eighteen." Randy concluded her history of Jordana's childhood. "Emma would've liked to lock her away, hide her, as insanity was hidden in the old days."

"Where was her mother?" Patrick's hand clenched about the glass that was fortunately too heavy to shatter. "Surely she tried to protect her child."

"Ava is a good woman, but a weak one. Henry Daniel took care of her as if she were as much his child as his wife. When he died, Emma assumed control and Ava was no match for her. To Ava's credit, she did see that there was no physical abuse. Verbal and emotional abuse are more insidious and harder to fight. It was Jordana who finally had enough.

"They were at the Daniel town house in Atlanta, on one of the old woman's infrequent shopping excursions, when she ran away. Can you imagine the courage it took? A girl who'd never been allowed to mix in society or to go to school, who'd been kept a virtual prisoner, a blind child? Can you even begin to imagine the desperation that drove her to walk into the jungle of Atlanta?"

"You met her then? When she was desperate and running?"

Randy nodded abruptly, the memory as vivid as ten years ago. "She was crying. Silent tears, the blood of her soul. And she was dirty. God! How many times she must've fallen, stumbling from one place to another with no idea what to do or where to go. It was dark, a place where no one is safe. Even dirty, her clothes were too good for that part of town. When I first saw her huddled on a curb, I was sure she was a little rich girl who'd come slumming and maybe had a fight with her boyfriend.

"I had troubles of my own and figured hers were stupid in comparison. I stopped to ridicule and stayed to help. But whatever I did, Jordana did more. In the midst of her own misery she listened to mine. Then, out of the blue she offered me the kind of life I never thought I could have. I was a stranger. I could've been an addict, a thief, a murderer. But her instincts can be uncanny, and she trusted me from the first. She offered me an education and a home for the baby I was carrying."

"In exchange for this?" With a gesture Patrick indicated the kitchen and the work she did there.

Randy shook her head. "In exchange for nothing. I do this because I like it. It's what I want to do."

Beyond the archway Jordana laid down her guitar. Her hair spilled like bright silk over her shoulder as she laughed with Cassie.

"So you went with her to school in Switzerland." He spoke to Randy, but his eyes were full of Jordana. "Then you came back to Georgia. You had an education, could've had some sort of career. Why did you stay?"

"Why would I leave? Where would I find another person who would do what Jordana did for me? She took a pregnant black girl off the streets and made her into a lady. She gave Cassie a chance for a better life than either of us had. Would you leave anyone who'd done as much for you?"

Patrick shrugged aside her question. "What about Cassie's father?"

"He doesn't figure in this. He was out of my life before I found out I was pregnant. I was in love, he was in heat, but for a time he was everything I wanted, on any terms. From a wiser perspective, I reckon it as his loss."

Jordana's arms were around the child—long, graceful fingers guiding stubby, clumsy ones over the guitar's strings in halting chords. Turning, blocking woman and child from his sight, he narrowed his gaze on Randy. "Considering your own experience with a rogue, why do you think Jordana needs one in her life?"

"Because the alternative is worse." Randy's reply was immediate. Whatever her doubts of Patrick, in this her conviction was unshaken. "She's stopped reaching out. She's closing in and down, becoming a recluse. As Emma Daniel would want." Randy spit the last, her black eyes snapping with fury. "It has nothing to do with courage. It's just that she is, by nature, retiring and time and circumstances enhance our shortcomings, as well as our virtues. Jordana needs someone who won't let her slip away. Someone who's involved in life and will take her with him into it."

"If she gets hurt, it could be worse. She could withdraw even further."

"She'll have memories. That's better than nothing."

"Is it?"

"Yes!" Randy was emphatic.

Patrick sipped from the glass for the first time, then set it down. He stared into it. "Jordana needs permanence in her life—she deserves it. I'm not the permanent sort, not yet, not for a while."

"Then leave," Randy said brutally.

Liquid splashed against crystal. "I can't."

Randy's hand covered his. Her harshness was gone as quickly as it had come. "I know," she murmured as she watched his gaze turn to Jordana. "I know."

When Patrick rose and walked into the night, Randy stared after him, certain for the first time that Jordana's heart wasn't the only one at risk. "Patrick McCallum, you're a stubborn man! Too stubborn to admit the truth."

She was smiling when she poured the rest of his drink down the drain.

"Good night, Jordana."

As Randy swept the child away to bed, Jordana sat thoughtfully, listening to their chatter. Then, laying aside her guitar, she rose, going unerringly through the den and the kitchen to the garden terrace. Though he denied it, Patrick's trouble was far more than restlessness. He was tangled in the trap of her foolishness, and it was time she set him free.

For a while their relationship had gone well. Patrick became first a frequent visitor and then a houseguest, coming and going as his schedule permitted. In an idyllic world of their own making, they had walked and talked and laughed, learning about each other. Not just critical things, but the trivial things that made each more real to the other. Out of dissimilar lives they discovered common ground, and forged new and unexpected interests. From Patrick she learned of those distant countries she would never know. From a world traveler, a personal view missing from Cassie's videos. In turn, he'd shown an interest in her life, in the things that mattered to her, her music, Soar, needy children, her garden.

He knew the flowers by name now, even considered the four-o'clocks more than weeds.

They'd become friends, but it was a friendship with a bruised ego and bitter vanity as its basis. Patrick had been drawn to her, then, rebuffed, had pursued her with a single-minded goal.

She had flown from him, rejecting every advance. Until it was he who turned away from her. Then the vanity she hadn't known she possessed had wanted him to want her. Vanity needed to believe the woman who could not see was as desirable as the woman of mystery, encountered in an Atlanta restaurant.

Ego and vanity, with desire their common goal, with an inevitable end. But the timing was wrong.

Her mistake, Jordana admitted as she stepped into the night air. She had dared him, with no understanding of what it meant, even less of what she was asking of him. She had thrown down the dare he couldn't refuse. Intending to soothe the hurt to her own conceit, she had fought fire with fire. But it was she who was burned.

She moved across the terrace, guided by the subtle protests of a chaise not meant for one so large. "Patrick." She touched his shoulder and knew from his reaction that he hadn't heard her approach. "I know you want to be alone, but, please, may I join you?"

He caught her hand in his, holding it. He'd been curt with her earlier, but there was none of the pouting, wounded pride of the women of his world. "How do you do it? You move through the darkness and through a world that must be seven kinds of hell every minute of every day. Yet you're always fair and kind and even tempered."

"Not always." She drew her hand from his, needing distance to say what she must. "I've been neither kind nor fair to you."

"When have you been unkind or unfair?"

"With this situation." She found a chaise and, with the grace learned of difficulty, settled into it. "With the notion that I could be like other women, as desirable as a normal woman. I was too angry to consider the consequences, for either of us. I was too angry to think at all."

"What are you saying, Jordana?"

Clasping her hands before her, she turned her face away, letting a current of night air cool her fevered skin. She hadn't expected it to be so difficult to release him from an unspoken promise. She hadn't expected to fall in love with him. "I suppose I'm admitting my own arrogance and apologizing for it. There's nothing more to hold you, but because you're a kinder man than you'd ever admit..."

"Do you really believe that it's kindness that keeps me here?" With the tip of a finger he turned her face to him. "Are you really that naive?"

His finger traced the line of her cheek. The shock of it skittered like lightning down her spine. "It isn't naive to know kindness is part of it. You don't want to hurt a friend."

"Is that how you see yourself? As a friend?"

His fingers were threading through her hair with a mesmerising rhythm. "I had hoped we were friends, Patrick. I thought we had come to be, until..." She had to struggle against the shiver that took her breath.

"Until my moods?" he supplied, not surprised by her perception, only its interpretation. She was naive and far too trusting. "Jordana, love, a man doesn't hiss and spit like a tomcat because he doesn't want a woman." He smiled, a grimace of derision at his own dilemma. "Just the opposite."

"But you've been a perfect gentleman."

"Every minute of it has been agony."

"Why, Patrick?"

"Why?" he muttered. "Because every minute I wanted to do this." His lips brushed over her eyelids, closing them, feeling her lashes brush against his skin like the flutter of the wings of a butterfly. He drew away only long enough to cup the back of her head with his palm, his fingers burying in her hair. "And this," he whispered under his breath as his lips skimmed over hers, teasing them, not moving away until he heard her soft sob of surrender.

"Most of all, this." Anger flared within desire. At himself, for promises made and promises broken. As he covered her body with his, molding her softness to the hard demand of lust, his kiss was urgent. His mouth possessed her, his tongue taking hers as her lips parted in a gasp. His hand found the opening of her shirt, and then her bra, brushing it away as if it were gossamer. His palm cupped her breast, letting it fill his hand, feeling a deep satisfaction as the nipple hardened, as his own body had, with desire.

There was little gentleness in his purpose as he stroked her body, determined to drive her as mad as he. With his touch he taunted her, with his kiss he teased, until her body was taut and hungering for more.

Jordana, who had lived by her senses, was sure that now she would die by them. Nothing in her life had prepared her for Patrick, for his exquisite assault on her heart and soul. Nor for the caress that left her shivering with delicious pleasure yet strangely unfulfilled. Her body hungered and his touch was sustenance. She thirsted and his kiss was wine, but neither was enough.

When she thought he could drive her no further into dementia or enchantment, his hand stroked the length of her denim-covered thigh and back again, lingering at the hollow of her belly. Her sudden cry arched her body as his mouth closed hotly over her nipple. His tongue curled and teased, his suckling sending a quivering warmth pulsing through her and a storm gathering beneath his caress.

"Patrick!" Her hands were in his hair, keeping his mouth at her breast, straining for more with the instinctive undulations of her body.

With a shake of his head he was moving away, rearing up from her. The lost heat of his body left her chilled as the memory of his kiss warmed her breast. "Please," she cried, and reached for him. Drawing him back to her, she felt first the imprint of his body, every hard plane folding intimately against every yielding curve, then the lave of his tongue at her nipple, stroking, seducing, and at last the suckle that set every fevered sense spiraling into one need.

The grate of the zipper of her jeans was like thunder in the darkness. Creatures of the night stopped their secret rustling, waiting, listening, while only the halting breath of a man's desire for a woman and hers for him disturbed the night. Patrick's hand blazed a trail for his mouth, over her face, her throat and her breasts, paying homage again to the succulent buds of her nipples. Then down her midriff to her belly, lingering at her navel, his tongue dipping into the well of sweetness as his plundering poised on the brink of an intimacy she'd never experienced.

His cheek rubbed over her belly, the stubble of his beard like the rasp of a kitten's tongue, his breath hot against her flesh. "Has anyone ever made love to you?"

She shook her head, unable to speak, but in the darkness he sensed what he already knew.

"Then this is wrong," he said heavily. "It shouldn't be like this for you. Not for your first time." As if he were watching a man in a dream, he gathered her clothing about her, zipping and buttoning it tightly until every tempting secret was hidden.

Patrick McCallum had never in his life denied himself. He had never had to wonder, as he did now, if cold showers really worked. Swinging his legs over the side of the chaise, he rose abruptly, setting his back to the lovely picture she made in the moonlight. With her hair tossed and tumbled about her, and her lips swollen with his kisses, she was tempting. Too tempting to be a virgin long, if he didn't move away.

In long strides he walked to the edge of the pool, but not even the waft of cooling air that gathered at its surface could wash away the scent of her. It clung to him, like a subtle embrace drawing him back to the brink of desire. Kneeling on the rock ledge, he scooped a handful of water, splashing it over his face, but not even the biting odor of chlorine could wash the memory of her from him.

Dragging his cupped hands through his hair, he let the water sluice down his face and over his shoulders. And then again and again, until his shirt was soaked and plastered to his body. The cool splash of the water offered no relief. After weeks of celibacy, when the loveliest and most willing of women could not tempt him, he needed Jordana. Only Jordana.

Even Maeve Delmari, with the agile mind of a scholar, a body worthy of a centerfold and the skills of a courtesan could not interest him. In the past few weeks Maeve had become a nuisance. She took his gift of rubies, but refused to believe their affair was done. With every wile she pursued him, appearing unannounced at the offices of McCallum American or the restaurants where he dined. As she grew more desperate, her penchant for daring clothes grew more exaggerated. Where once her daringness was governed by good taste, now she sought simply to tease. Low-cut dresses that had always revealed a generous swell of breasts now barely clung to their pointed tips. Sheer blouses over naked nipples and skirts slit to the hip—horrors more suited to Hollywood than Atlanta—had left him immune and coldly disgusted.

Maeve flaunted herself, offering every carnal delight, yet it was an innocent woman dressed in cotton and denim who set his pulse throbbing.

The sound of her footstep was lost in the splash of the water; her touch at his shoulder came without warning. Instinctively he flinched, jerking upright and away, forgetting. The sudden move sent her reeling, and only his quick reflexes kept her from falling. His fingers folded about her wrist as she caught her balance, but long after she needed him he held her.

"I'm sorry," he managed at last.

"Why are you sorry, Patrick? Because I nearly fell? Or are we back to the chorus of a tired old song? Are you sorry because I'm blind?"

"If it gives you any satisfaction, Jordana, tonight proved your point, in spades. Being blind has nothing to do with how desirable you are."

"Then why didn't you make love to me?"

"Virginity carries a price I'm not ready to pay."

The price he wasn't ready to pay was love. The essence of every woman's dreams. Even of a younger Jordana. She'd come to send him away. Instead, she would settle for half a dream. The love would be hers alone, secret and undeclared, and when Patrick was truly gone, she wouldn't love again. Randy was right; loving once was better than never. "Virginity isn't a commodity to be bought or sold or bartered. It's neither a gift nor a curse, and I'm no more nor less because of it.

"I'm a woman, with a woman's needs." She laid the flat of her palm on his chest; beneath the soaked shirt his heart pounded with a hard and steady rhythm. "I need you, Patrick."

"Don't play with fire, Jordana. You might get burned."

"Too late." She lifted her face to the moonlight, her smile a little sad. "I have already."

He didn't know what she meant—he didn't want to know. It was enough that she wanted him. "Then come with me." Dragging her against him, pressing her breasts to his wet chest, he bent to kiss her. "Come with me to Scotland," he muttered against her lips. It was the last thing he'd intended, but if she had the courage for that, then she would have the courage for the day when it ended. "Come with me and for a while we'll have the world. I'll give you sunrises and sunsets, days of flowers and sunshine, nights of love."

"Yes." Jordana was rising to meet his kiss, though she knew the love he promised would be with his body, not from his heart. Tears she wouldn't let fall glittered on her lashes in the moonlight. "I'll go with you, Patrick. Anywhere."

"No!" As he realized what he'd asked, that she'd agreed, his denial was startling, mercuric. His hands closed over her wrists. A trapped man struggled against the walls that were closing in. Angry disgust, coiled and waiting like a viper, struck swiftly. As he dragged her hands away from him, the cold sweat of sickness washed over him. Patrick McCallum had never been a weak man. He controlled his own destiny, answered to no conscience but his own. He bowed to no one.

No man or woman in his adult life had left him questioning himself or his motives. No one mattered enough.

Her unquestioning trust was too new to him. The old need to protect himself from the currents she stirred in the depths of his heart was too strong. For the first time in a long while Patrick McCallum was confused and uncertain. Like a cornered animal he lashed out at the source of his confusion.

In the white light of the moon, his face was a reflection of his fury, and not even her look of speechless bewilderment could cool its rampage. "You would, wouldn't you?" Teeth were clenched, his grip over the fragile bones of her wrists unrelenting. "You would go with me anywhere, do anything. Asking nothing, giving everything. Not even protecting yourself in your pretty innocence."

A muscle flickered in his jaw as he hammered home his point with a lie. "I don't need your innocence or you. I need a woman who understands. One who's been around enough to protect herself. Do you understand what I mean by 'protect,' Jordana? Or are you too innocent to have considered it?" When she flinched and paled, he knew he'd scored a perfect hit. Virgins had no need to protect themselves. The bitter reminder only fueled his anger. "I thought as much.

"I need sons someday, legitimate sons, not red-haired bastards to remind me of foolish indiscretions." She suffered his cruel barb silently. Only her eyes, sparkling in the moonlight, betrayed her hurt. Patrick's swift, irrational anger shriveled like a weak and ugly thing cringing in the presence of gentle strength.

The bewildering need to hold her and kiss away her tears came as swiftly as the anger. The perverse pride that would not let him, as irrationally.

"I'm sorry, Jordana. For everything." His voice was gentle now. His hand hovered at her cheek, within inches of one last touch. Then, as if her very nearness hurt, he jerked away, his fingers curling into a fist. Taking another step back, he murmured, "Forget Scotland. Forget me."

With one last look he stepped into the night.

Six

"Yes, Patrick. I realize you left for London rather abruptly. No, I haven't heard from her." Rafe tucked the telephone between shoulder and cheek, reaching for pad and pen. In his bold hand he had made short notations as he listened to the barrage of instructions. "It's worth a try." Then he asked, "What the devil is a four-o'clock?" Listening, he made a note on his pad, and when the surprise faded from his face a grin began.

"Are you sure the florist will know?" Another note. "Is a flower that only opens in the evening suitable for a bouquet? Does it open or close when it's picked?" Rafe winced, holding the telephone away from his ear, and he grinned in earnest. When Patrick fell silent, he resumed their conversation. This time for Rafe it was tongue-in-cheek.

"Why the hell did I think you'd know? Because in a matter of weeks you've become as expert on flora as you've been on fauna for years." Wincing again and grinning, he waited. "Yes, I know, bad joke. Today's modern woman wouldn't appreciate it. But at the moment there isn't a woman around.

"Yes, Patrick." Rafe sighed, laid paper and pen aside and listened once more to his friend. Before he was through he wondered what ever happened to the days when a bouquet was simply a bouquet, not a matter of thirty minutes of instructions by trans-Atlantic call.

Ivy and daisies and lilies and something called four-o'clocks? A sheaf of gardenias or roses would be simpler. "The woman can't see, why should it matter what flower you send her?" Rafe wondered when anything with Patrick had been simple. Drawing the pad forward, he underlined the strange name. If Patrick wanted Jordana Daniel to have four-o'clocks, she would have them.

"I'll deliver them in person, promptly at four as we agreed. Now, if you can drag your mind from your lady-love, how are matters in London? Will Sheffield agree to the deal?" Flowers for Jordana were put aside, but not forgotten. "Difficult? What's difficult?" Rafe's pen tapped the desk, and his grin disappeared. "Longer than you expected. How much longer?

"Days, even a week." In a merger of this magnitude, a week wasn't long, nor a month or half a year. Ordinarily Patrick would know that and accept it. With little grace at times, but more than now. The difference was Jordana. The Scot was head over heels into something over her. Rafe wasn't sure if the something was love or lust. Whichever, he'd never seen his friend like this.

"Yes," he said for what seemed the tenth time and with great patience even for the cool Creole. As a friend he agreed to be Patrick's peace emissary, to lay the groundwork for the mending of some fences. In the meantime

Patrick suffered ungraciously the need to remain in London a few days more. "I'll see to it. Promptly at four."

After the call Rafe considered the changes in his friend, questioning if the Scot himself understood them. In their conversation, in which returning to Atlanta figured prominently, Rafe had refrained from reminding Patrick his original plans were to return to Scotland. Imagining the resulting explosion, Rafe spun his chair from the window that overlooked Atlanta.

"Where is he?"

Looking up from his notes, he realized there was a very modern woman around. Maeve Delmari had dressed with decorum today. "Patrick, do you mean?"

"Of course, Patrick!" Maeve snapped. "Who else would I mean?"

"Who else, indeed?" Rafe murmured, checking his temper. "How did you get in here?"

"I told Mrs. Hedley you expected me."

"I see." He'd neglected to inform Mrs. Hedley that Maeve Delmari was no longer welcome in the offices of McCallum American. He made a mental note to correct his oversight.

"You didn't say where he is."

"No, I didn't." Rafe watched as she moved into the office. At the window she drew a cigarette from her handbag, flicking a gold lighter at its tip. Drawing deeply and exhaling, she crossed her arms and stared over the city.

"I knew it wouldn't last." She inhaled again, her long, red-nailed fingers curling about the cigarette.

"You knew *what* wouldn't last, Maeve?" Rafe's green gaze was cold. He had little patience with men or women who entered into an arrangement, fully cognizant of the rules, then rebelled when those same rules no longer suited.

"This newest little liaison of Patrick's, naturally."

"Naturally," he drawled. "On what do you base that bit of insight?"

"I heard you. You were speaking to Patrick. Taking your orders like a good little boy." Maeve crossed the room and, leaning over his desk, she ground out the cigarette in a spotless ashtray.

Rafe let the sneer pass. He'd had too many years of dealing with antagonism to be bothered. Maeve was lashing out; a gilded dream had escaped her. "What orders, Maeve?"

"For the gift. What is it this time? Diamonds? Emeralds? Even for such a short time, Patrick would be generous."

"Try flowers, Maeve."

"Flowers?" A startled frown marred her beautiful face. "Why would he send her only flowers?"

"Because it isn't over. I suspect it's just begun."

With fumbling fingers she lit another cigarette. The smoke was rising from it as she crossed her arms, hugging them close. "Flowers today, maybe, but it will be jewels tomorrow, or the next day, or the next."

"Not this time."

"Yes." The word was a soft hiss, and the cigarette was flung angrily away. "Patrick will have his fill of her, then he'll come back to me."

"You aren't that stupid, Maeve. You know from his history that once an affair is done, Patrick never goes back."

"He will this time." From her purse she took a flat velvet box, placing it on his desk. "I won't need these, for I promise you, he'll be back."

"You're overestimating yourself."

"And you're underestimating me. Patrick's stayed with me longer than with any other woman."

"Six months isn't long, and he was out of the country for most of that." Rafe felt only pity for the woman who couldn't believe her charms weren't as enduring as she thought. Maeve wasn't the first woman to think she could keep Patrick, but she promised to be the hardest to discourage. "Forget him, Maeve, and take these." He picked up the velvet box, tossing it closer to her. The rubies rattled inside it. Red stones, her favorite color. "Consider them his last generous act and enjoy them. Get on with your life, he won't be back."

"He will!" Furiously she slapped the box from the desk, sending it skittering over the carpet. With a bitter smile at the necklace spilling from the box and one for Rafe, she strolled to the door. Bracing her hand on the knob, she paused. "You know him better than anyone, but this time you're wrong. He'll be back. She'll have the jewels, whoever she is and wherever she is, and I'll have Patrick back."

The click of her heels was lost in the normal sounds of the workday. Rafe rose, closed the door left open with more effect than a slam, scooped her cigarette from the scorched carpet and discarded it. Crossing to the spill of rubies and gold, he gathered them from the floor. At a wall safe he spun the dial through an intricate combination, and dropped them inside. Safekeeping, until Patrick decided how to deal with them and with Maeve.

The next half hour he spent in conference with Mrs. Hedley, clearing his calendar for the favor Patrick had asked.

"They're lovely!"

The clock had just struck four, introductions had been properly made and, as Rafe promised, Jordana stood at her doorstep holding Patrick's bouquet. After the long drive from Atlanta, the flowers weren't in the perfect condition he would've preferred, but as he watched her bury her face in them, he knew all that mattered was that they were from Patrick. If she could've seen their wilted, drooping heads, she wouldn't have cared.

Rafe began to understand Patrick's enchantment.

"Four-o'clocks!" The days of limbo were forgotten. Jordana's face was alight with more than pleasure over flowers. "He was so angry when he left, yet he remembered."

"Of course, he didn't forget," Randy said dryly from her post in the foyer. "How could he when you and Cassie are so nuts over a flower that's gotta look like a weed to a supposedly sensible man like Patrick? Anyway, since when does going off in a snit impair the memory? Seems to me that it's more likely the opposite. A bad conscience usually is accompanied by an exquisite memory." Not as eager to forgive as Jordana, she added, "At least I hope it was."

"The misunderstanding was as much my fault, Randy."

"Was it?" Randy was skeptical. "Somehow I doubt it. But the flowers are a nice gesture." Despite her grudging tone she nodded her approval. "Give them to me and I'll find a vase while you take our guest inside."

Jordana was accustomed to Randy's gruff manner. She only smiled and relinquished the flowers. Hooking her arm through Rafe's as if they were old friends, she led him to a room that was as warm and welcoming as his hostess.

"When I called, I didn't think you would see me." Rafe had taken the seat across from her.

"Why would you think that?"

"First of all because I'm a stranger, Jordana. All of this, the mystery, the seclusion, precludes strangers. And because I represent a man you've quarreled with. Patrick didn't explain, but, judging from his actions, it's more than a lovers' misunderstanding.''

''But it was only a misunderstanding of a sort. One easily rectified. I wasn't certain Patrick would care, but his flowers and your presence must mean that he does.'' If any anger or hurt lingered, it was swept away by the thoughtfulness she suspected was as new to Patrick as love was to her. She was happier than she'd been in days. The smile she turned in Rafe's direction included him in that happiness. ''I suppose we are too reclusive to welcome strangers, but you're not a stranger. You're Patrick's friend.''

She said it as if it explained everything. When Rafe saw her face light up at the mention of Patrick and heard the sound of her voice when she spoke his name, he thought perhaps it did.

''Patrick's told me so much about you,'' she continued. ''I feel as if I know you.''

''He's spoken of you, as well.''

''Has he?'' She laughed delightedly, then sobered in thought. ''I suppose he speaks of all his...'' Bowing her head and clasping her hands tightly in her lap, she laughed again. This time it was a self-deprecating sound. ''I don't know what to call the other women in his life, or myself.''

''Don't call them anything, for he never speaks of them. Not as he has of you.''

''I must seem silly, but this is new to me. There's never been anyone like Patrick.'' She turned to him. It was nearly impossible to believe her lovely eyes were sightless.

''There's never been anyone like you for Patrick.''

''Because I'm blind?'' There was nothing coy in the question, only an honest need to know.

Rafe was seeing in her what Patrick must. Truth and honor and trust, rare qualities that from Patrick's earliest memories were foreign to women. ''Your sight isn't important, Jordana. It's what you are that matters. You're an honorable woman. There haven't been many in Patrick's life. Except for the first woman in his life, honor never mattered, until you."

"The first one?"

"His mother."

"She hurt him?"

The telephone rang, as Rafe had been expecting. "That will be Patrick, calling from London." His mission done, he rose from his seat. "I'll say goodbye now."

"Don't." Her voice was low, urgent. "Rafe?" Her hand extended in the direction of his voice. When he took it, she clasped his tightly. "Don't leave. There are things I don't understand. Things you can tell me. I'm not asking that you betray Patrick's trust, just that you help me understand."

The telephone jangled again and again, then it stopped. From the next room Randy Taylor spoke to Patrick.

Though he'd always trusted Patrick's judgment, Rafe had come fearful he would find a glamorous, mysterious woman playing to the hilt the natural, wholesome image she projected for the camera. He'd been concerned that for once the man he loved as a brother had been beguiled. That this woman was not what she seemed, and Patrick would be hurt.

An unparalleled reaction, for, before Jordana, he hadn't thought Patrick could be hurt.

As he looked down at her now, Rafe feared that one wrong move in this fragile time, and both would be hurt. If he could keep that from happening, he would. "All right." He folded her hand in both of his. "I won't leave. While you take your call, I'll see if Randy can be persuaded to give me a glass of the lemonade Patrick is so fond of."

Jordana smiled gratefully. As she lifted the receiver, gratitude turned to joy as she cried simply, "Patrick!"

Hours later in London, Patrick paced the length of the drawing room, viewing the rich appointments as a wild animal would a gaudy circus cage. A cage, however grand, was still a cage, and the beast confined was left to stalk its little space.

Calling her had been a mistake. The difficult weeks since their quarrel—his quarrel with himself if he were honest—had been oddly bearable for a while. But only, he admitted now, because of a fatalistic certainty that he'd destroyed any hope of being more to her than a cruel and hateful memory. He had accepted that, had told himself he didn't care, that he was better out of the madness.

Then a drift of perfume had reminded him of a silly flower, and hope reared its dauntless head.

From that moment he had no choice. Had he ever really? With Rafe's help and a bouquet that had probably been a dismal failure, he had to try. He had no idea what to expect, and then he heard her voice.

"Why don't you hate me, Jordana?" His question rose futilely beneath the vaulted ceilings. "You should!" But there had been no hate in her. Only an assumption of a share of a mistake. Patrick McCallum, stunned cynic, was as leery of an honest woman as of the schemers.

"What do you want, Jordana?" The walls of his solitude had no answers.

"It was ridiculous to call." Dragging his hand through hair that waved crisply over his forehead, he turned to pace again, berating himself. He should simply have gone back, arriving unannounced, to collect what was his for the taking. "The whole bloody thing is ridiculous. I should've made love to her when I had the chance. Should've tumbled her there on the chaise by the pool. She wanted it as badly as I. I should've brought her here with me, and taken her at my leisure. When I'd had enough, I could've sent her home, with her pocket stuffed with jewels. Then I wouldn't be mooning like some sick calf."

Or stalking like a beast in need of a mate.

Patrick looked to his address book lying open by the telephone. There were women listed there who would come to him if he called. He wouldn't call. He wanted a woman, badly. Not just any woman.

He wanted Jordana.

Her name was a litany, a chant, trapped in his mind. There was a cure, and he would have it. With an angry gesture he stripped off his tie and flung it aside. "To hell with courting and romance! To hell with virgins!" Tomorrow, as soon as the plane landed, he would go to her, and no matter the hour, she would be his.

He was tempted to cancel his meetings and order the plane readied immediately. Common sense prevailed.

His decision made, he expected a clearer mind. Tomorrow would come soon enough. Going to his desk, he planned to immerse himself in reports. Just when he thought he'd found the perfect solution and could put her from his mind, he remembered the sound of her voice over the phone, her delight in his flowers.

"Dammit!" Papers were slung carelessly aside. Why should a silly bouquet of weeds mean more to Jordana than furs and jewels, simply because they were from him?

What did it mean?

He was on his feet and across the room with a drink in his hand before he realized it. He stared down at it, wondering why the devil he'd poured it. With a shake of his head he set it aside and began to pace again. At the window he stopped, the hard planes of his face softening as he looked through the night to the profusion of an English garden. Within the glowing circle of stately brass lanterns, colors were richer, textures deeper. In the moisture-laden air fragrances would be intoxicating.

He could imagine her there, a Summer Girl, dressed in white, captivated by a feast of the senses. She would love every flower and every shrub. And if there were lowly, scraggly weeds with wonderfully fragrant blossoms, she would love them, as well.

"Jordana, lass," he murmured softly, in his distress the rolling, throbbing accents of Scotland strongly apparent. "What am I going to do about you?"

As he sank into a nearby chair and buried his face in his hand, he was remembering very well what he wanted to do.

"Why were you surprised Patrick decided to come back tomorrow?" Jordana's hand rested on Rafe's arm. When he'd expressed an interest in seeing the infamous flower in its natural habitat, she'd invited him in for a tour of the garden.

"Earlier he'd said he needed a few more days. I suspect a week or two would be a better estimate."

"He changed his mind. Is that unusual?"

"Changing his mind? No. Leaving a critical deal undone. Yes."

"Surely he knows what he's doing."

"He has before."

"You mean before I came into his life?"

"Of all the women, through all the years, he's never lost his head as he has with you."

Jordana's heart began a slow, heavy throb. Her throat was dry, and her breath was drawn in a ragged sigh. "You would know," she said in little more than a whisper, "wouldn't you?"

"Better than anyone." Rafe matched his step to hers. "We met here in the States in military school and we've been friends for twenty-five years." He felt the jog of her arm as she sidestepped a jutting stone.

Hearing his surprise, she explained ruefully, "No miracle, or ESP. The stone has been there for years. I've run into it often enough that to save my shins, I finally learned to remember where it is." She dismissed her accomplishment, returning her attention to Patrick. "How old was he?"

"Twelve. The school spent the next six years educating Patrick and taming me."

"You make yourself sound like a juvenile delinquent."

"Just a wild kid. Patrick and I had our share of problems. Patrick's mother was an unfaithful witch who deserted her family. His dad couldn't cope with losing her, so he sent Patrick away. Not because he didn't love his only child. He did, so much he couldn't bear for him to see the disintegration. But Patrick knew. Since he was such a big kid, everyone seemed to forget that he *was* a kid. He was expected to handle her desertion and the separation from his father like an adult. He was never allowed to act like a child."

"Except with you," Jordana observed with new insight into Patrick and his friendship with Rafe. The hurt and pressure would've been enormous. Even a wild kid who understood would be a godsend.

"Yeah, except with me. I saw that being away from his father wasn't sparing him anything. He had a foot in two worlds. He was a kid who needed his dad, and nearly a young man who thought his dad needed him."

"Did he blame his father?"

"Never."

"Only his mother." And he hadn't loved or trusted a woman since. A boy of twelve had stood alone, learning harsh lessons, with only another child to care. Jordana released a long breath. No matter his size, a hurting child was never too big to be held and loved.

"Patrick's father died when he was sixteen. He was twenty-two before he could bear the hurt of returning to Scotland. For years he tried to deny it, but Patrick is a Scot and Scotland is his home. He knows that now."

Yes, Jordana agreed, Patrick was a Scot, and not even the many years in America could wipe all trace of Scotland from his speech. There were still the gentle nuances. She heard them in every word, stronger when he was wary, or angry. "When he returned, the bond you forged in school survived," Jordana said, understanding.

"Neither of us had brothers. The first year we scratched our wrists with a penknife and became blood brothers." Absently Rafe brushed a fallen leaf from her hair. "We've fought together and laughed together. If we'd been a different sort of man, we would've cried together." Then in a half mutter, he continued, "Maybe we have, in our own way."

Strolling through the shadows, Jordana was silent. The image of a lonely boy who couldn't trust because he'd been betrayed lay heavy on her heart. But he had trusted, and he hadn't been alone. He had Rafe. Gratitude welled inside her for the man who walked at her side, as he had at Patrick's.

"We were children, but the bond has lasted," Rafe continued. "I owe him more than I can ever repay. When I nearly lost my life, Patrick kept it for me."

An odd choice of words that Jordana wanted to understand. Recognizing a familiar scent, she knew where they were. "There's a bench by the wall. Patrick's favorite place in the garden. Would you sit for a while with me?"

Rafe had been lost in the maze for the past ten minutes. With a marveling shake of his head he asked, "How did you know?"

"The roses. The bench was placed here because Patrick likes them." Letting him guide her over vines and around a small ornamental pool, she sat on the bench and waited. There was more to the story, and a reason for the telling.

A bullfrog, frightened into silence by their coming, decided they were no threat and resumed his thrumming croak.

The bench creaked beneath Rafe's weight. "Patrick had just begun to recoup the family fortune. We were flying home after closing the deal that made it certain. Our plane went down in an isolated part of the Appalachians, and the pilot was killed. I sustained internal injuries and what we thought was a concussion. Patrick's leg was broken, with shattered bone puncturing the skin.

"I was confused, but ambulatory. Patrick fashioned crutches out of branches, insisting we couldn't wait for a rescue that might never come. It was winter, the foliage was gone from all but the evergreens, but the going was rough. Within an hour he knew I had more than a concussion. Later we would know it was intercranial hemorrhage. I was barely lucid, my left arm and leg useless.

"Patrick hadn't complained but he was in agony. With every move the bones were grinding, cutting his flesh. Night was coming, the temperature was dropping, soon we would freeze. I knew enough to understand that I wasn't going to make it. Patrick had a chance. He could move faster without me. He wouldn't go. Instead, he found a small cul-de-sac and dragged me there. With our backs to

the wall and surrounded by the fires he built, we wouldn't
freeze.

"I spent the night alternating between delirium and
sleep. Patrick worked, tending the fires, fashioning a
travois that would let him drag me and keep his hands free
for his crutches. By morning I didn't care. He cared, for
both of us."

Rafe stopped. The memories still hurt; the pain was in
his voice. Jordana touched his arm lightly and, when his
hand covered hers, folding it into his grasp, she felt his
appreciation for her empathy.

"I don't remember anything after that morning." There
was a rawness in him that time could never ease. "I thank
God that I don't have to remember what he went through
getting me down that mountain. How many times he fell.
How many times he got back up again."

He was crushing her hand, but Jordana would not pull
away. What was an aching hand when Patrick suffered so
much?

"The doctors wanted to amputate his leg. It was in-
fected, the bone was a mess. He wouldn't let them. He
wouldn't give up on himself, just as he wouldn't on me."
Rafe's laugh was a caustic bark. "We were a pretty pair for
months, with our cuts and bandages, my shaved head, his
braces. In the long run I faired better than Patrick. He
won't allow himself to limp, but the leg still hurts him at
times."

"Like all his hurts, he keeps it inside." Jordana was re-
lieved the pressure on her hand had eased, but she didn't
draw away. "You told me this story for a purpose, Rafe."

He didn't bother to deny it. "I wanted you to understand how deeply he cares. If he didn't, he couldn't be hurt
as badly as he has been. He's a difficult man, Jordana, but
if you love him, he'll be worth the difficulty.

"I was with him the first time he saw you. I've never seen him react as he did then, nor as he has now. Patrick's emotions are strong and deep. When he admits them, no man could have a better friend. No woman a better lover."

He traced the line of her jaw with his knuckles. "When he's difficult, remember, he loves you."

"No, Rafe."

"*Yes*. I wasn't sure myself, but listening to all of it, hearing it as a whole, and knowing Patrick, what he's like, what he feels..." Rafe shook his head, surprised at his own ignorance. "It's the answer! The obvious answer."

"No!" Jordana turned her face away.

"Jordana." With a finger at her chin he turned her back to him. There were tears shimmering on her lashes. "Don't be afraid. You love him. I saw it in your face when you were so delighted with his peace offering. He hasn't admitted it yet, but he loves you. That gives you a power over him no other woman has ever had."

Jordana wanted to believe that Patrick loved her. She wanted to believe more than anything in the world. The power Rafe spoke of frightened her. "I don't want power over Patrick."

"I know you don't, but love itself is power. To enrich or to destroy. The day Patrick tells you he loves you, you will have won."

"This isn't a war, Rafe."

"It is. It's your war with the past, for Patrick."

"What do I do?"

A tear spilled from her lash, and Rafe wiped it away. "Be yourself, follow your instincts."

"I don't want to hurt him."

"There are never any guarantees on that, Jordana." Taking her hand in his, he drew her to her feet. "I've taken up enough of your time. I should be getting back to the city."

Jordana gathered her courage. "What time does Patrick's plane arrive?"

"I won't know until I check his flight plan. But I'd guess late in the evening."

"I'd like to be there when he gets off the plane. I have a place in Atlanta that's rarely used, but if you'll give me time to pack a bag . . ."

"We both have until tomorrow evening, Jordana."

Meeting Patrick's plane would take every ounce of her courage, but, if he could cross an ocean for her, she would be there when he arrived.

Seven

Patrick stepped into the terminal, moving at a deliberate pace. Deplaning passengers scurried past him, a human current rushing to other destinations, other pursuits, other people. He was surprised by the quiet engulfing the concourse. In the years since he'd taken a commercial flight, he'd forgotten the night traveler was a different breed: the jaded, weary from the long day; the neophyte, subdued by the dark and waiting sky.

Some spoke in whispers. Some drowsed in their seats, sweaters and jackets drawn close against the artificial chill. Over them the unforgiving lights burned down, leaching away the mysteries, leaving only harsh reality.

He had forgotten, or perhaps he'd never seen.

Plagued by his own fatigue, his own realities, he wondered what he was doing here rather than at the jet port his company used. "Or London," he growled, "as I should be."

Flexing an aching shoulder, he studied those who stood idly by, searching for the driver Rafe would've sent. His eyes met the slanting glance of a handsome woman. She made no secret of her interest in an auburn-maned giant whose passions seethed barely beneath the surface. A smile quirked her lips as she smoothed her skirt. Patrick's eyes moved over her indifferently, dismissing what she offered. Her smile faltered and turned cold.

As he brushed past her, her scent was heavy, a cry of darkness and sin. He ached for sunlight and innocence.

As he searched the concourse for the elusive driver, his temper flared. He'd been as irritable as a wounded tomcat for days. It added little to his good humor that the company jet had developed engine troubles at takeoff. His first instinct had been to charter another. Only the need to prove to himself, if not Jordana, that he had at least a modicum of control prevented it. But what had he proved when he'd caught the first available commercial flight, then spent hours cramped in a seat not designed for his size?

With a strangled growl of impatience, he was swinging about, intent on finding the nearest bank of phones when he saw her. Stopping in midstride, he was hardly aware that the man half a step behind had collided with him.

"Hey, mister! Who do you think you are? You don't own the..." Registering the massiveness of the target of his ire and feeling the Arctic sweep of unseeing eyes, he swallowed the rest of his tirade. "Uh, sorry," he muttered, and fled.

As if the little man had never existed, Patrick's gaze returned to Jordana. It was like seeing her for the first time all over again. He wasn't prepared for the golden loveliness, the aura of gentleness that even the ruthless lights could not destroy. He was not prepared for the greed that blazed in his gut like an inferno. Not for the angry, bitter envy twisting through him when Rafe leaned to her, whispering, touching her cheek with his fingertips.

Watching them through slitted eyes, he saw her smile and nod, setting the white gold of her hair tumbling from her shoulder and down her back. As her laughter rose like a silver bell on a clear day, Rafe wrapped an arm around her, and drawing her to him, kissed the top of her head. In that moment, as he moved toward them, Patrick almost forgot that Rafe Courtenay had been his friend for more than twenty-five years.

He almost forgot that he had no claim to Jordana. That he wanted none.

Stopping before them, an arm's length from her, he was conscious of everything about her and of Rafe's touching her. His face was bleak as he faced the only man he called friend.

"Rafe." His nod was abrupt, his greeting curt.

As if waiting for its cue, in rapid succession his world tilted then righted itself. Rafe, ever a friend, a friend now, was moving away with a wicked grin that told its own story of mischievous amusement, and Jordana was surging toward him with a look of radiance. Instinctively his hands shot out, taking hers, steadying her in this rare, unthinking move. Standing in the busy thoroughfare, with a human tide parting about him like a river about a granite tower, he was concerned only with Jordana.

"Patrick!" Her hand curled tightly into his. He was troubled; she heard it in a single word. "Your plane was delayed, we were worried. Are you all right?"

"I am now." He was hungry for the sight of her. He had been from the moment he left her with the bitterness on his tongue and pain in his heart. No ocean separated them now, and if he stood here forever, he wouldn't tire of looking at her.

"Are you?" Jordana asked softly. The hurt was still there; she heard it deep in the timbre of his Scotsman's burr. A hurt that came from the battle he fought with himself, from betrayal, from memories carved in the heart of a man-child. Memories and hurt that had lain dormant until, on a sunlit day, he had come into her life.

She had done this to him as much as the mother she hated and the father he had loved. Taunting him with her reckless pride and wounded vanity, she had bound him to her when the honor neither betrayal nor hurt could destroy warned him to leave.

Drawing his hand to her mouth, she brushed her lips over his knuckles, wishing she could ease the pain a mother should have kissed away. The hurts of a child had become the hurts of a man. A bold, magnificent man, and the kiss she would give him was not the kiss of a mother. His hands were rough and warm against her lips. Without thinking, she touched her tongue to him in a caress of a lover.

"Jordana." He murmured her name, slipping his hands from hers, lifting her face with a curving finger. Her smile faltered, her lips trembled and golden lashes lay heavy over the bright glitter of tears. Patrick's teeth clenched, stifling a sound that might have been a groan. He was no stranger to tears of anger or petulance, but no one had ever cried for him. He wanted to hold her and kiss away each precious drop, to wrap himself around her, keeping her safe.

The need was so powerful he had taken a step closer when he knew he dared not. If he kissed her, he would not stop with her tears; then who would keep her safe from him?

A harried traveler jostled his arm, grumbling something uncomplimentary about Patrick's choice of rendezvous. Patrick swung about in anger, shielding Jordana, only then remembering where he was. He needed to get her out of here.

"Rafe."

"He's gone."

"Gone?" He looked to the wall where Rafe had lounged in that graceful, negligent manner that was his alone. No green eyes laughed back at him. No brow quirked in sardonic amusement. There was no trace of the Creole. "What the hell!"

"He never intended to stay."

"Never intended... What about you? What about transportation?"

From the pocket of her slacks she took a key. "He left you this and took a cab."

"Just like that? He left you high and dry?"

"Just like that, he left me where I want to be."

When he'd seen her with Rafe, he hadn't stopped to think how strange it was that at this hour she would be miles from home, with a man she'd only met yesterday. He hadn't stopped to think that she was here for one reason alone, to meet his plane. He'd been too busy being stupid and jealous to think at all.

He was thinking now, seeing what only a fool wallowing in his own misery would have missed. She had cut herself off from all that was familiar, leaving the security she had created for herself, venturing into a world she could not see. To be where she wanted to be.

"With me." Those who had been bested by the ruthless Patrick McCallum would not have believed the tenderness in his voice. Patrick himself would not have believed if he'd heard. "You want to be with me."

Only the gawkers who had begun to gather, pointing and whispering as they recognized Jordana's face, kept him from kissing her then. He settled for touching her cheek, cradling it in his palm. "Do you know what you're saying? What it means? What it *has* to mean?"

"I know, Patrick. I've known, I think, since the first time you kissed me."

He took her arm roughly, his angry stare sweeping over the onlookers. "We have to get out of here before I make a scene."

With his fingers curled above her elbow and his big body clearing the way, she was rushed through the living circle, down the corridor and ultimately to the parking deck. Patrick didn't speak again or touch more than her arm until they were seated in Rafe's roadster.

"Now," he growled, reaching for her, dragging her hard against him.

His fingers threaded through her hair, tugging her head back, but the kiss she hungered for never came. His hands moved down her body, and his forehead rested on her shoulder. He was so still the thud of his heart against her breast was like thunder. Winding her arms about him, she stroked his hair, letting his auburn curls tangle around her fingers. Crisp, bright, like autumn leaves, Randy had said.

Jordana smiled. She had only her imagination, but in it he was beautiful. More beautiful than anything in her life.

His heartbeat slowed to a strong, measured rhythm. He took a deep breath, his head lifted, and his hand slid up to frame her face. "Now," he said again hoarsely. "Now, Jordana."

His mouth on her was hard, uncompromising. Even with the moment of calming there was no mercy. He wanted. He took. Had he not, she would've given freely. She had long ceased to worry of the consequences or the future. Right or wrong, she had today and for today, she had Patrick. As she gathered him closer, her lips parted to his, meeting passion with love as she went without reservation into uncharted land.

He moved away, only inches, touching with his fingertips the face that had smiled at him from every newsstand, from his thoughts. She was warm and real beneath his touch as he bent to kiss her again. A kiss more desperate than the last, less than the next, and the next.

He groaned as he rolled away from her. Gripping the steering wheel, he stared into the darkness. "After that there's no way I can drive for hours and keep my hands off you."

Her bridges were burned; there was no going back. She wouldn't if she could. A bouquet of bedraggled flowers had put her fate in his hands. "I'm not going home."

"Jordana." He had no idea what he should say or do.

She heard the soft trill in her name. That, more than anything, was evidence that the dashing Scot was for once a lover out of his element. She touched his hand. "Stop fighting, Patrick. The battle's over for both of us. You've learned to live with my blindness. Tonight I'm asking you to forget it. In the darkness and in your arms, it won't matter. I'll be the same as any woman.

"You've made no promises. I expect none. I simply want tonight." Her throat was as dry as dust. With her hand gripping his, she whispered, "I want you."

Patrick's hand turned in hers, his fingers lacing through hers. He was silent. Only the release of a long-held breath shattered the quiet desperation. A curse, a sigh, then gutturally he asked, "Where?"

Jordana pulled away from a grasp that was suddenly excruciating. He was not going to make this easy for her. Was he subconsciously trying to drive her away, trying to force her to make the retreat when he couldn't?

She would not retreat. Could not.

"The Daniel town house." Hearing the voice of a stranger, she repeated the name of a street and the address. "I haven't stayed there in years, but it's kept in readiness for..." She was surprised by the swift lancing of pain. She'd thought herself immune. "It's kept as my grandmother liked it, but she never uses it." Explaining the old woman's perversity, she added, "It's mine and my money that keeps it."

With a soundless curse meant for Emma Daniel, Patrick turned the key in the ignition and sped through the concrete switchbacks of the parking deck to the street.

The interior of the house wasn't what he expected. Jordana's home was warm in its simplicity, comfortable in its style. This one was a study in cold perfection. From a portrait over a mantel a haughty-eyed woman with a ramrod back and a pursed mouth stared down at them.

Emma Daniel. Patrick's arm tightened about Jordana's shoulder, drawing her closer. He knew she didn't need to see to be aware of that cold, disapproving gaze.

He stared into the face of the woman whose ignorant pride had nearly destroyed one more beautiful, more generous. Even now Emma's small-mindedness reached out for Jordana. She injured with contempt, expressed by shunning a house that waited like a gift for her.

"She doesn't matter, Patrick. Not to us."

He didn't question that she knew what he was thinking. "You're all that matters." Bending, he swept her into his arms, proving his point with a kiss that left no room for doubt. Barely lifting his mouth from hers, in an undertone he demanded, "Your room? Where is it?"

"Beyond the stair at the end of the hall." With her cheek resting on his shoulder, she drew from his strength, letting the heat of his body ease the chill of her memories. She'd brought him to this house for a reason. It was here a frightened, desperate girl had changed the course of her life.

Ten years had passed, but it seemed fitting that she return tonight.

Yes, she thought, fitting. She sighed and, content with her decision, put her memories aside. Her heart was thudding, not with fear or the shame she'd once been taught, but with the quiet elation of love as she clung to the man who was the light in her darkness.

Closing the door to Jordana's room was like stepping into another world. Turning with her in his arms, Patrick saw the imprint of the woman she had become. Books, the special books she would need, were lined in shelves, and the carpet was thick and soft, the wood smooth. No drapes covered the doors that led to a small, railed balcony. Trapped in a dreary house with a dreary woman, she had found a way to bring the sun and the world into her life.

"Amazing." He let her body slide down his, his hands curving about her waist as she found her footing. He saw the strength here, the carving of her own niche in the face of impossible odds. He had never admired any woman as much as this one. Nor desired one so much.

"Amazing," he murmured, taking her lips again, feasting as a famished man. Then he backed away, forcing a restraint that was nearly impossible. He'd crossed an ocean and a city in a fever for her. She deserved better than the quick tumble he'd planned, better than a rutting stag easing his own needs at the expense of hers.

This was her first time. He would make it her best.

When she reached for him, not understanding his withdrawal, he took her hands in his. "No, lass." He kissed her palms. "There's no hurry. We have all night."

Jordana shook her head, not understanding. He'd been so urgent, now he was backing away.

"Trust me, Jordana."

"I do. I will."

"Then I'll get our bags from the car. While you have a long, hot soak and relax, I'll see what has been laid in the kitchen for us." He touched his finger to his lips, then to hers.

He was gone then, the door closing behind him, leaving her in a room newly polished and cleaned. Old memories were swept away with the dust; now it waited for the new.

She'd gone obediently to the bath, meaning only to wash quickly, but she hadn't reckoned with the fatigue of the hours spent driving to Atlanta with Rafe. Nor the tension in waiting for Patrick. As heat unknotted muscles and a favorite fragrance soothed her mind, she slipped into a languor that was sensual and wicked and delicious.

Stretching her arms over her head, feeling the cascade of scented water over her breasts, she knew this night would be the most perfect in her life. She was smiling when Patrick tapped on her door and entered. She made no coy show of cowering and covering; the time for modesty was long past and she was too honest to pretend.

"This was in your..." Patrick stopped in his tracks, sucking in a breath as if a fist had just hit him squarely in the chest. The flimsy negligee in his hand was forgotten. He hadn't expected her to be quite so heartbreakingly lovely.

Dreams were for fools and love a weakness. He'd lived his life vowing he'd be neither weak nor fool. Yet as his gaze devoured her, he knew he'd lived a lie. Rose-tinted bubbles drifted over the water's surface, clinging to her golden skin. Sparkling bangles for a dream. And he was a fool.

But love? He closed his eyes, blocking her from sight. His mouth was a thin slash in a pale face. Denial shuddered through him. Turning to leave, he remembered the bit of lace crumpled in his hand. A garment meant for a dream. Only a dream. Flinging it from him, he said, "This was in your luggage. Wear it."

Speechless, Jordana sat in the fragrant water, wondering if all men were mercurial, or only men who struggled to be patient. If it was a matter of patience, Patrick's was nearly at an end.

Rising in a cascade of fragrance, she reached for a towel.

A door closed and Patrick looked up. The room was dark, with only a spill of moonbeams to light it. He'd been right. As it caught the light the amethyst lace was the garment of dreams. Jordana was beautiful, with her hair falling like a veil of silver and gold over gossamer. His Summer Girl, dressed in the color of summer twilight.

Crossing to her, he drew her with him to the open door and the tiny balcony. The night was still as he poured the wine. There was fruit and cheese on a small table, but as she accepted her glass, he knew it would be left untouched.

"To dreams." He touched his glass to hers.

"Dreams." She sipped the wine, savoring its delicate flavor calmly, while inside the smoldering desire strained to be free. A stranger to these rituals, she fought a quiet battle and waited. Patience, she counseled, and smiled wryly over her wine.

Patrick saw the curving of her mouth and the darkening of her eyes. Her breasts rose in a sigh, the lacy décolleté dipping over their fullness. Taking her glass, he set it aside with his. "It's time, Jordana."

"Yes." The time for patience ended as she moved into his arms. He smelled of soap. His shirt was open, his skin damp. He'd not only found his way to the kitchen, but to the shower in the master bath, as well.

Her fingers were unsteady as she ran them over his chest. Unsure at first, then bolder, exploring, learning the wonders of the male, of Patrick. Feeling the power of muscles that tensed at her touch. He was solid, unyielding, from flat abdomen and slender waist to broad chest. He was steel and sinew beneath the rigid flesh. At his shoulders she hesitated, only briefly, before pushing his shirt from her path.

With a groan Patrick shrugged it away. Letting his arms stay at his side, he gave her silent access to his body. He'd known the practiced touch of many women, but Jordana's was like the first. New, innocent, a delightful agony, almost more than he could endure.

Her fingers fluttered down his arms, down the swell of the biceps and the forearm. Brushing over his ribs, she lingered again at the heavy musculature of his chest, a palm over his heart. Intent on her revelations, her face had grown somber. As the rhythm of her own heart blended with his, her expression softened, understanding the torture of her touch.

Sliding upward, her hands circled his throat, traced the line of his jaw and cheek, then buried themselves in his hair to draw his lips to hers. He reached for her and stopped, allowing her to guide. Holding himself taut, he let her tease his mouth with hers. Giving only what she took.

Jordana moved away. The space between them pulsed with a fiercer need. From arm's length she traced a path with a fingertip from his throat to his waist. "I think you must be the most beautiful man."

"You're beautiful, Jordana, not I."

"You are to me."

"You've no comparison, how can you know?"

"I don't need other men to know. I don't need anyone but you." The button at his slacks slipped free even as his hand was closing over hers to stop her.

"God, no. Not here. I don't think I have the strength for more." Swinging her into his arms, he held her close, gathering his wits. "There are better places for the rest." Striding across the room, he took her to the bedside.

She was an illusion in shadowy gossamer, too beautiful to be real, but when he slipped the lace from her, she was warm and very real. Drawn by a memory of clinging, rose-tinted bubbles, he stroked her breast and she trembled.

"Do you tremble because you're frightened, Jordana?" he asked her softly.

"No." She swallowed convulsively but did not move away from his caress. "I'm not frightened of you. Never of you. You're a beautiful man, Patrick, inside as well as out."

"No..." he began, but the words were lost as he looked down at her. For Jordana, goodness was beauty, and to her he was beautiful. "God help us, I hope you're right," he muttered as he drew her down with him.

Driven nearly to the brink by her touch, her words, her trust, he began a slow, sweet seduction.

He knew how to tease, how to torment, driving desire from one feverish plane to another. He knew where to touch, where to kiss to draw the tears of passion that left a woman wanting more, needing more, but unsure she could bear it. He knew how to reach that deep, unthinking craving, turning it into the madness that magnified every touch and kiss, every beat of her heart, every stroke of his body.

Passion for passion's sake. He'd never wanted more. Never needed more than its animal satisfaction. He'd never wanted the wonder nor the miracle, but he wanted it now.

It would be his gift to her.

He was gentler than he'd ever been. Kinder. Caring more for her pleasures than his own. But kindness was its own reward, for she was attuned to him, sharing, learning, sensing his needs, giving back as he gave to her. She murmured his name, and it was like a flame burning in him. His hard, possessive fingers stroked through her hair and down her body. Heart-shattering hurts that had shaped them into solitary beings were forgotten. They were fire and flame trembling on the brink of a world where neither had ever gone.

Almost reverently he kissed her. His words were halting, a whisper against her lips. "I'll only hurt you once, Jordana, then never again."

The night was wine dark. The cry of a nighthawk rose from the garden, joining with hers. Then, like the hawk the pain was gone. There was only Patrick as he taught her the last of rapture for which the first was made.

Music woke him. Notes of quiet passion from the strings of a guitar drifting on the quiet of dawn. Beyond the balcony the sky was gray with only a touch of crimson that preceded the blaze of the rising sun.

Dressing in slacks, on bare feet he followed the sound. He would find her as he had many times, sitting cross-legged on the floor, bending like a willow over her guitar. Face rapt, eyes closed, her fingers would be straying over the strings, turning her thoughts into melody.

The rough tile of the hall was cool beneath his feet as he stopped in the open arch of the great room to listen. There was sadness in the notes as she sat playing beneath the portrait of the woman who had called her music the meanderings of an idiot. The sorrow faded, underlying tones of contentment woven through it growing stronger. The pace did not change, nor the passion, but Patrick knew. With Jordana's music, one needn't be an expert to know.

When she stopped, the last note fading like an echo, he spoke. In his voice was the emotion he'd heard in her song. "It was for her, wasn't it? For Emma."

Jordana turned to him, clutching the guitar, an old one that had been hers as a child. "For her." She smiled up at him. "And for me."

Patrick sat beside her on the carpet, wondering what the deathly prim Emma Daniel would think of a half-naked giant sitting with her granddaughter who wore only his shirt. For a moment he wished with all his heart that she was there to see. He wished that she could hear the song that had been both a sad farewell and an affirmation of strength. The song would have haunted her. He knew it would haunt him, long after he was gone from Jordana's life.

It would haunt him, but she would never play it again. Even he was sensitive enough to understand that some things were meant to happen only once.

He wanted to hold her, but settled for resting his hand lightly on her shoulder in a gesture that told her he was there to listen if she wished it. If not, he was simply there.

Ducking her head, she touched her cheek briefly to the back of his hand. It was her way of thanking him. One more expressive than words. The silence lengthened. Jordana stirred, laying the guitar aside and clasping her hands before her. When she began to speak, he had to strain to hear.

"She was always ashamed of me. I was ugly, my music was an idiot's pastime. I should be kept away from the public eye so no one would know. An education was wasted on me. I was imperfect, an affront to all the Daniels past and present. God willing, there wouldn't be any future Daniels, for then they would have to be mine. *And* thank God no one would ever find me attractive enough to make that horror possible."

She lifted her face toward the portrait, and it was uncanny that her eyes seemed to meet Emma's. "I was rarely allowed to come to the town house. Someone might see me. When I was eighteen, for some reason I can't even remember, I was allowed to come. On the last day of our stay I walked away. It was a frantic bid for freedom and for a life. I hoped that if I proved her wrong, she would be proud of me. She never was."

Patrick's stare fastened on the portrait, hatred flashing in his eyes. "She was a fool. She's a fool still."

"Perhaps I should despise this old house, but I don't. I love it. I found the courage to change my life here." Covering his hand at her shoulder with her own, she said, "It seemed right to bring you here tonight."

He remembered the melody she'd played, a wistful yearning for something, then letting go. He marveled at the strong heart that could manage it. "I know." Taking both her hands in his, he kissed her. "Are you hungry?"

Jordana laughed, a wonderful sound. "Starved."

As the sun rose they were sitting primly across from each other on the balcony. Beyond the heavy railing a cluttered garden drooped and died from neglect, but they were too happy to care. Sharing the same glass of wine and nibbling from the same wedge of cheese, they laughed at everything and nothing, like children. Until they fell silent, realizing that their hunger was not for wine or cheese.

When Patrick took her hand, Jordana was rising to him. As they walked arm in arm to the bed, Patrick remembered the garden.

Jordana should have flowers.

As she opened her arms to him, he promised himself she would.

Eight

"*Nothing* is impossible." The telephone was wedged between shoulder and ear as Patrick spun his chair from the window to the desk. With a yellow pen he circled a list of names on a pad before him. "I don't recall asking the cost."

Rafe appeared in the doorway of the office. Seeing that Patrick was occupied, he started to leave. With a silent gesture Patrick indicated he should stay.

"The timetable isn't negotiable," Patrick continued on the telephone. "Either you can do the job or you can't. In which case, Mr. Osaka, there are others who can." The yellow pencil was flung on the desk. "I *have* a lot of money, Mr. Osaka."

A rare statement that lifted Rafe's brows. Taking a chair, he listened in undisguised amusement.

"By the weekend." Then, exasperated, he said, "What you do, Mr. Osaka, is go yourself instead of waiting for delivery. Yes, go yourself. You have the list exactly as I gave it to you? Roses and ivy. Later gardenias. By the weekend. See that you do."

"Well," Rafe said when the telephone clattered down. "That was an interesting conversation."

"I see you enjoyed it." Patrick met his gaze levelly, without a trace of humor.

"What in the world are you doing, Patrick?"

"What does it look like? I'm planning a garden."

"For Jordana?"

"No," Patrick said sarcastically, "for my own amusement." With a glare, he continued, "Of course, for Jordana."

"With Mr. Osaki."

"Osaka."

"Whoever." Rafe shrugged. "What's going on?"

"It's a long story."

"We have five minutes. Most long stories can be condensed to that."

When he was done, Patrick realized it had taken less than that. Supplied with the bare bones of his plans, Rafe could deduce the rest.

"So, for now, Jordana's at home." Rafe's grin had disappeared. "What does the inimitable Randy think of your plans for spending weekends with Jordana here in Atlanta?"

"She hasn't decided whether to kiss me or cut my heart out, but she's agreed to work with the decorator in refurbishing the Daniel house."

"While you attend to the garden."

"Along with Mr. Osaka."

"Jordana knows none of this?"

"About the house and garden? No. That I intend to be a part of her life? Yes."

"For how long."

"I don't know. I never do."

"This one's different, Patrick." Rafe said it quietly.

Again the blue, level gaze met Rafe's. "I know."

"She doesn't fit the pattern. Nor your plans for the future, I might add. Jordana's a far cry from the plump little partridge you've always planned to settle down with. The mother of the children you need. By whom you expect to be bored to tears while you keep your code of marital fidelity."

"That hasn't changed." It couldn't. Heirs were necessary for the entailed lands in Scotland. The only thing his father had loved more than the land was his wife. The land Patrick could keep for him.

"It could if you found a woman you could love."

"I won't."

Rafe didn't argue. It would be useless. "In the meantime there's Jordana."

"Until I get her out of my system," Patrick retorted, putting an end to the conversation. "I assume you came in here for a purpose?"

"I have the information you requested on Jordana's financial situation and particularly on Soar, her recording company."

"Which is?"

Rafe read from scribbled notes. "A private company. Stock held only by Jordana and Randy, some in trust for Cassie. Self-supporting but nonprofit. Everything earned is turned back into it."

"Possibilities?"

"Good." Rafe tucked his notes into his jacket. "If anyone wanted them to be. Everyone concerned seems content to keep it as it is."

"It's no financial threat to Jordana?"

"Quite the contrary. Even with the funds she earns as a model channeled into it, it's no threat. Henry Daniel left his little girl more than comfortable. The old biddy you were nervous about didn't fare so well."

Patrick was surprised. "How do you mean?"

"John Daniel skipped over his wife, Emma, in favor of his son, Henry. Henry left everything he had to his daughter, Jordana."

"Then Emma is dependent on Jordana's generosity. At the same time, Jordana is beyond Emma's less-than-tender mercies." Though his smile was cold as he considered the alternative, Patrick relaxed. Henry Daniel was a wise man. He'd protected his daughter as best he could. "There's no way the old woman can get her hands on anything Jordana has?"

"None. She's already tried. Didn't work."

"That's what I wanted to be certain of. Thanks."

"It's a matter of public record. The only trick is knowing where to look. If I didn't know, my source did. Your lady's safe." He tossed a sheaf of papers on the desk. "The report on Briggs Publishing. Looks promising."

Patrick flipped through the papers. "We did a good day's work in acquiring this."

The day he had first seen Jordana.

"The London Project could be as good," Rafe predicted. "If we pull it off."

"We will." Patrick glanced at his watch. "I'm leaving for London within the hour."

"Returning when?"

"By the weekend."

"You expect to make that much progress in three days?"

"Enough that I can finish up by telephone from here."

"Just how long will you be staying here, Patrick?"

"That remains to be seen."

"You were planning some time in Scotland."

"It can wait."

"Scotland can wait? Since when?"

"Since Jordana."

"I see."

"Do you?"

"Enough to know that no matter how you protest, this time is different."

"Different approaches for different women, Rafe. You know that as well as I. Jewels for a woman like Maeve. Flowers for Jordana. A sterile high rise for one. A home for the other. Little things. That's the only difference."

"I wonder if she will understand that. Somehow I don't think so."

"You're wrong. She understands perfectly. Jordana told me herself that in the dark, she was like any other woman. It's what she wants."

"Is it what you want, Patrick?"

"Why wouldn't I?"

"Because you pursued her for reasons you're denying now. Because she's unlike any woman you've known."

Patrick stood and picked up his briefcase. "I have a plane to catch." Striding across the room, he stopped at the door. "I repeat, my friend, in Jordana's own words, all women are the same in the dark."

"You play the bastard well, Patrick."

"Who said I was playing?" With a mock salute he stepped through the door.

"Aren't you?" Rafe murmured when he was alone. "To paraphrase a master, the man doth protest too much."

"Mr. Courtenay?" A very young clerk stood barely inside the office, a perplexed look on his face. "There's a Mr. Osaki on line three."

"Osaka, Richard," Rafe corrected automatically.

"Yes, sir." Richard was too harried to question. "He keeps going on about a garden and a week. He wants to speak to Mr. McCallum about something called six-o'clocks."

"Four-o'clocks," Rafe corrected, this time with a grin.

A look of relief crossed Richard's face. "Then you know what they are? I'm not losing my mind?"

"I know what they are and you aren't the one who's losing his mind." Rafe's grin grew to a chuckle. "I'll handle Mr. Osaka." At Patrick's desk he lifted the receiver. "Mr. Osaka. Rafe Courtenay, McCallum's CEO. I'll be handling this project while Patrick's in England."

Waving the curious clerk away, he listened to Mr. Osaka's protests. "I know exactly what they are. There's no mistake."

A pause, a struggle for composure. "I assure you, Mr. McCallum always knows exactly what he wants." *Sotto voce,* he added, "At least as a rule."

A longer pause, for the duration of what he assumed was incredulous Japanese. "You know what they say, Mr. Osaka, one man's weed is another man's flower."

Sitting on the desk with his long legs stretched before him, Rafe waited again. "They don't?" His laughter was barely contained now. "Well, perhaps they don't really say it here, either. Just the same, I would suggest you go against your better judgment this time and put in the four-o'clocks. Trust me."

Replacing the receiver with exaggerated care, Rafe sprawled in a chair and propped his feet on the desk. "So, my friend, all women are the same, are they?"

Then, with his hands folded at his waist, he laughed.

"Stand still," Randy commanded around a mouthful of pins. "I swear, Jordana, when you're nervous, you wiggle as much as Cassie. This is how you tore the hem out of this dress in the first place. Slacks would do better on the helicopter anyway. Helicopter!'' She mumbled, ''What next?''

"I have to wear this dress, Randy. Patrick's been in London nearly two weeks longer than he intended and it's his favorite.'' A frown crept over Jordana's radiant face. "It looks all right, doesn't it?''

"It looks terrific, but a burlap sack would look good to him if you were in it. I'm just surprised it still fits. He hardly lets you off the telephone long enough to eat.'' Rising from her knees, Randy added drolly, "That particular telephone bill must rank up there with the national debt.''

Jordana clutched at Randy's hand as she smoothed a wrinkle from the waist of the blue dress. "Come with me. Cassie would love the helicopter ride, and while you're in Atlanta you could take her shopping.''

"Now, wouldn't Patrick McCallum just love having us along as extra baggage?'' Randy wrapped her arms about Jordana. "Butterflies?''

"Maybe he's changed his mind. Maybe he won't be there when I get there.''

"There's little chance of that.'' Stepping away, she smoothed back a curl that had spilled from the combs that held Jordana's hair in its sleek coil. "You don't have anything to worry about. Not as long as you're careful.'' Then, addressing the subject that most disturbed Jordana, she said, "You packed the pills?''

"Yes.''

"You haven't missed any?''

"No.'' A flush crept over Jordana's cheeks. "It all sounds so cold-blooded and calculated. So ugly.'' She bowed her head, then, needing to face her thoughts, lifted it again. "Randy, what am I becoming?" She spoke in a whisper. "I never thought I'd be any man's mistress."

"Mistress! Shush that talk," Randy scolded. "Sounds like something your grandmother would say to make you feel guilty for grabbing at a little bit of happiness. If there's one thing this world doesn't need it's two people who think like Emma Daniel. Anyway, a mistress is a kept woman. That's the last thing you'll ever be.

"We all make the choices we have to make. We live with those choices and their consequences. That's all the more reason to know there's nothing cold-blooded and ugly about being careful, and don't you forget it."

"I know you're right, Randy. Everything inside me tells me you are, but I still feel like a..."

"Stop it. You're a smart, sensible woman, Jordana Daniel, in love with a lusty man. That's all."

"I do love him."

"I know." One look at her face and the whole world would know. Except Patrick McCallum, who would only see what he wanted to see. For a moment Randy was overwhelmed with doubts of a different sort. She had gambled on Patrick. Now she feared Jordana's heart was a price too dear to pay. As the faint flutter on the horizon became a deep, chopping roar, she wanted to pretend the approaching helicopter was only a monstrous dragonfly to be shooed away.

Instead, she walked with Jordana to the open lawn, holding her cold hand, trying not to see the color drain from her cheeks. Who would most regret the chain of events set into motion by this day? Randy wondered. Jordana Daniel? Randy Taylor? Or, surprising thought, Patrick McCallum?

Then it was too late for wondering. The helicopter landed, and Rafe was crossing the lawn for Jordana. By the time they reached Atlanta, the plane from London would have arrived and Patrick would be waiting.

The helicopter barely touched down on the tarmac of the heliport before Patrick was there. His arms engulfing her, he swung her from the cockpit with a laugh and an unintelligible shout. When they'd cleared the rotor and the buffeting backwash, he set her on her feet, only to drag her back into his arms.

Jordana was disoriented. Her keen senses were no match for the roar of the engine, nor the swirling force of dust and debris stirred by the flying blades. She was lost, caught in an unfamiliar hurricane. Then Patrick was calling her name in the instant before his mouth covered hers, and a world faulted with misgiving was forgotten.

With his fingers tangling in her hair, he taught her that desire wore many faces. So tenderly that his lips were a whisper, his kiss drew her into a web of longing that was still and deep and hushed.

He'd been a man of contrasts, impassioned yet remote. A burning flame, a wintry frost. One consuming, one beguiling, as the dark side of his lust ravaged the secrets of her body. But this kiss, his promise to cherish, awakened passions that would endure beyond the flame. Beyond the frost.

Doubts fell like shackles. In surrender a gentle heart stepped beyond the last reserve, daring whatever love would bring.

Patrick sensed the change. His mind did not understand, but his heart recognized passion, fearless, exquisite. Yielding without reserve. To him.

Only to him.

"Jordana, I..." A hand clamped over his shoulder, and he spun about, his face flushed, angry. "What the hell!"

"Patrick." Rafe struggled with a grin and lost. Struggled again and won, pointing at the helicopter that hovered in readiness to take off. "Duck."

Blue eyes locked with green. Anger faded. Patrick drew a breath. His lashes fluttered down, then up again. His lips quirked wryly. "Too late."

"Yeah." Rafe's gaze did not waver.

Patrick nodded. Their hands clasped. Creole and Scot, saying more than words. The Scot was first to grin.

An engine revved, stirring dust into a whirlwind. In a gesture as natural as breathing, Patrick shielded Jordana's body with his, not even thinking to curse the pilot.

"Impatient jerk." Rafe said it for him. "He'll pay for that little trick." Then, with a flashing grin for Patrick, and a muttered "Luck!" he was sprinting for the helicopter with blood in his eye.

In the wake of the departed helicopter Patrick swooped to kiss Jordana again. Keeping her close, he muttered into her hair, "I missed you. And if you didn't miss me as much as that kiss tells me, I don't want to hear it."

"I missed you, Patrick." Her cheek lay beneath his heart, its steady beat her anchor. She'd followed as he willed, where he willed. Caught in a cacophony of sound, voices blended into the high, thin shriek of machines or were lost in the deep vibration that shattered the sky. The stench of gasoline and solvents lay heavy, like oily smoke, in her lungs. Nothing was familiar. Only Patrick. Without him she was lost. "I missed you more than a kiss can say. More than I knew."

"Did you, now?" His voice was husky, soft. "As much as that?" He was moving away, meaning to tease. The male ego gratified, until he saw her face and the lingering bewilderment she'd tried to hide. With his palm he cradled her cheek. The sultry day had drawn a fine sheen over

her, and her skin was damp against his. Strands of white
gold had tumbled from her heavy chignon. A streak of
dust clung to the hem of her dress. She was ashen and
flushed at once. Her eyes, the dark rich blue with flecks of
lavender that created amethyst, were shadowed, and not
even the sun could light them.

Disheveled, fragile, but magnificent, as with grace and
spirit she refused to break under his clumsy demands.

Patrick closed his eyes, listening to the chaos. In the
workday furor natural to the heliport, he heard the shriek
of engines and breathed the stench of fuel. Without sight
they were magnified. To the young, imaginative mind they
could become a scream of banshees, the reek of a nether-
world. For a mature woman thrust suddenly into an alien
world it meant confusion, dread of a misstep, a loss of self-
reliance and pride.

This was the uncertainty of her life, the quiet fear she
must live.

He drew her to him, holding her, rocking her against
him, understanding at last the withdrawal Randy feared.
"Sweetheart, I didn't think."

He'd grabbed and tugged, trundling her about like baggage, concerned only with his own selfish desires. Never
remembering this fast, furious life would, must, exact its
price in courage and strength. "A heliport is hardly the
place for... for anything." Kissing the top of her head,
letting the scent of flowers cleanse his lungs, he murmured, "Let a fool take you home."

Jordana went with him as the sun bore down and the
humid air rose from the scorched ground like steam. On
the fringes of the heliport, where concrete and steel ended,
the scent of newly mown grass was rich and thick, and a
hummingbird chittered in a tree. Far in the distance thunder rumbled, its sound distinctive, natural.

In the hot, sultry day, as Patrick drew her to him, murmuring soothing words, a storm no words could tame was rising.

A gentle rain had begun when Patrick stopped the car before the stately old Daniel house. The only clouds in the sky were miles away. Raindrops that spattered about them as they walked arm in arm from the drive to the house were warmed by the sun.

Patrick did not hurry. The rhythm of the rain was slow, easy, thrumming like the soft, low notes of Jordana's guitar. In the quiet storm, passions were strong and deep. And like the earth with its rich, dark scents rising about them, they were forever.

He stopped her a step away from the door and, when he turned her to him, raising her face to the rain, he saw she felt as he did.

"Patrick." She said his name softly, her fingers straying over his face. Her sensitive touch brushing over the furrows of fatigue, discovering the strain of his weeks in London. Patrick's life was as changed by this day as her own. As she had shaken free of old strictures, he had abandoned the code that governed his life. For the first time since a mother's betrayal of a beloved father, Patrick cared. He hadn't wanted to. He'd fought long and bitterly against it. A fight with himself.

Everything he was and believed resisted putting his heart at the mercies of another. Yet he had. It wasn't love as she would wish, but tenderness and affection from Patrick were as precious as love.

It hadn't been easy, this slow, tortuous defeat. Now he had come to her, risking his heart. She would give him hers. "Patrick," she murmured again, her fingers stroking through his wild, shaggy mane. Rising on tiptoe, she touched her lips to his, tasting the rain, tasting him. "I love you."

He was so still, so quiet. There was only the patter of raindrops falling about them. Jordana drew away, moving from the circle of his arms, waiting.

Patrick struggled for the breath he'd lost, his chest heaving, his fists clenched. He'd heard the words many times. But never like this. No woman had ever given them as a gift to be rejected or treasured, asking nothing in return.

Rain lay on her cheeks and clung to her lashes like tears, but her face was serene. Not even the ravages of the ordeal of the heliport dimmed its radiance. He touched her cheek, catching a raindrop on the pad of his thumb. It was warm from the sun, warmer still from her flesh.

"I know," he said at last. A part of him had known for a long time. He'd known when she made love with him. He knew it now and it frightened him. More than anything in his life had frightened him. His voice was ragged, drawn from the depths of confusion. "No one has ever loved me before. I don't know what to say... what to do."

Her fingers closed over his mouth. "Don't say anything. I don't need it. All I need is for you to make love to me."

"Yes." He swung her into his arms, and in his impatience sent the door crashing against the wall. The tap of his footsteps rang on new marble. The scent of paint and lemon oil dueled with the fragrance of flowers that filled every vase on every table.

He'd meant to surprise her with the changes wrought by harassed artisans driven by his long-distance direction. But he could wait for his surprises. He could wait for everything but Jordana.

In her room with her door securely shutting the world away, he set her on her feet. The only changes here were an antique guitar, old and fragile but still resonant and beautiful, and a small desk for Patrick. The only flower was a rose gathered from the garden beyond the balcony.

He knew they were there. The first he'd searched out and chosen himself. The second was from his home in Scotland, from his own room. The flower had been chosen at his direction, by Mr. Osaka, from the garden made for Jordana. He'd never admitted how important this homecoming was until faced with his own efforts to make it special. He hadn't realized that having her back in his arms would be enough.

Holding her, he kissed her, taking the love she offered. He teased with his lips and caressed with his hands, until her breath was like the sigh of the wind that danced beyond the balcony. He could feel the heat of her body beneath the dampness of the blue silk that clung to every curve from hip to turgid nipple.

As his kisses grew deeper and his hands roamed, desire that had smoldered burned with a torrid flame. When his lips followed the path of his hands, down her throat and over the slope of her breasts, her head was thrown back, her hands clutching at his shoulders. She murmured disjointed words, nonsensical phrases. When his mouth closed over her silk-covered nipple, her murmurs became cries, the nonsense his name.

Her fingers clawed into his shirt, the nails nearly piercing the fabric. As he leaned her back, his mouth made forays over the soft contour of her breasts, returning time and again to suckle, letting the rasp of his tongue over silk please her. They were thigh to thigh, hip to hip, their bodies straining against the bonds of clothing.

Jordana shivered and Patrick muttered eloquently. From the sound she knew it was Gaelic, and from his tone, a curse.

"You're cold! I've let you stand here in clothes that are soaking." He hugged her closer and laughed, a shaky sound that rumbled in her ear. "Clothed and dripping when I'd much prefer you naked." He tilted her head to look into her face, and what he saw there drew him back for another kiss. Against her lips he whispered, "Wait right here, exactly as you are, and we'll remedy both our problems. You'll be naked and warm and where you belong in a heartbeat."

Jordana's smile rippled over her mouth. She liked the sound of his laughter, but she missed his arms about her too much to laugh with him. She took a deep breath, breathed in the scent of roses. The room was different, changed. Or, she wondered, was it she who had changed?

She heard Patrick's approaching footsteps and the rustle of cloth. She hadn't realized that in the cool air of the house she had grown cold. When she reached for him, needing the heat of his passion to warm her, his hands closed tightly over her wrists.

His grip relaxed, but he did not let her go. "Don't touch me. Not yet."

Puzzled, Jordana was silent, but after a moment she nodded. When he released her, she let her hands fall to her side. As he commanded she stood pliantly while he slipped the combs from her hair, running his fingers through it time and again, combing the tangles from it. Her dress was next; the snap at the neckline opened, and damp silk slid down her shoulders and arms, clinging at her waist and hips before tumbling to the floor. She thought the long, dark stockings would be next. Instead, she heard the whisper of cloth, and the velvet roughness of a towel moved over her.

In his hand the towel became an instrument of delightful torture, massaging, caressing, buffing her body to a warm, vibrant glow. This time when she swayed and reached for him to steady herself, he didn't deny her. As she gripped his shoulders she discovered he was naked, his clothing stripped away before he came to her. He knelt before her. Slowly, carefully, the stockings were drawn down and, with her shoes, slipped away.

"No!" she cried, not certain she could bear it as the towel began to move again.

"Yes." Behind her, beyond the open door the sun still shone and the rain still fell like translucent threads. Against the light she was a gilded silhouette. With his gaze never leaving her face, he began his magic, seeking out secret places. When she wept, her body swaying like a reed, her hands burrowing in his hair to hold him, he whispered again, "Yes."

Grasping her wrists and with a turn of his head kissing the tender flesh of each, he rose, lifting her against him as he stood listening to the quiet. The rain had stopped, and when he took her to bed, there was only the hushed sounds of passion more gentle and yet more consuming than any before.

The deep, shattering rumble of thunder woke him. Jordana was no longer in his arms. He felt lost and empty, as sorrowful as the moaning wind that swept over the eaves, driving a new rain before it. A new roll of thunder began in a low growl, building slowly to shake the house. At the height of its fury, the single lamp that lighted the gathering gloom flickered and died. Instinctively he turned, meaning to take her back into his arms, needing to comfort her though she couldn't see the light or the dark.

His seeking hands found only the rumpled sheet, still warm where she'd lain.

"Jordana." His voice was lost in thunder that ran the gamut from a shrillness that nearly burst his eardrums to bass, felt more than heard. Throwing the sheet aside, wearing only a look of anguish, he called to her against the rage of the storm. Dragging a hand through his hair, he cursed himself and the weather. She'd been through enough today. Her strength had been taxed to the limit by the decisions he'd demanded, by the journey to a strange land where only he was constant. Now the weather conspired to frighten. He turned to revile the storm. As if in answer, lightning flared in the clouded darkness.

He forgot his curses when he saw her on the balcony, drawn in ebony against the bright fire of the sky. With her head thrown back and her hair flying in the wind that caught her laughter, she was a pagan goddess worshiping the elements. "My God! Jordana."

She was so beautiful and he was so afraid he could only whisper. But, as if by telepathy, she heard him. Or perhaps it was simply her sixth sense. When she turned to him, her eyes met his. She beckoned and, as he had so many times, he almost believed she could see.

"Patrick!" She took his hand in hers when he touched her. "Can you feel it? The storm! The electricity! The sounds are colors. All the colors of the rainbow. In the storm I can feel what my eyes can't see."

"Aren't you afraid?"

"Of feeling?" She was laughing and she'd never been more beautiful. "Never."

Catching her hair in his hands, he looked into the face of a woman who felt the colors of the storm. Who walked with fear and refused to be afraid. The woman who was the keeper of his heart.

"And of loving me?" he asked in an unsteady voice.

Drawing his hand to her mouth, she kissed his palm, her lips lingering. "No matter what it brings me, I'm not afraid to love you."

Patrick spoke then, in sweet, rolling Gaelic. Beautiful words. Words of love. Words he would someday make her understand.

The rain had begun again, harsh and hard and wind driven, and her need was as fierce as the storm when she drew him to her.

Nine

Patrick was first to wake. The night and the storm had passed. The day was shining, newborn, as was he. Watching Jordana sleep, curled against him like a kitten, he felt a contentment that wiped old hatreds from his heart. Her love had washed them away, replacing them with dreams he'd never dared admit.

In the sane light of day his doubts were of himself, not of her. He was too much the stranger to these emotions to trust that this overwhelming need for her was true and lasting love. He knew the price she'd paid, the principles she'd sacrificed in coming to him. She needed the words; he would like to give them to her. But he must be sure. With Jordana, more than anyone.

He'd never said I love you. Perhaps he never would.

Regret for all he would lose if the words weren't his to give tore at him with vicious claws, turning the sweet, languorous ache of passion spent to despair.

Careful not to disturb her sleep, he left the bed, padding on bare feet to the balcony. The Daniel town house was not one that marched side by side with countless others. It had the flavor of New Orleans, with a private, tree-shrouded lawn contained by grillwork and brick walls. Mr. Osaka had created a miracle. The garden that had been dying from neglect only weeks ago was luxurious and stunning. Roses in abundance bowed and dipped, their fragrance rich and wonderful in the currents that stirred the air.

Asian roses. He'd learned of them, their name and habits in his search for the most fragrant blossoms. Roses that would flower repeatedly through the summer. But not even Mr. Osaka could give him the wonderful June roses when June was so long past. He could only promise those ancient strains. Delicate flowers with the enchanting fragrances that hadn't been sacrificed in hybridizing the too-perfect modern rose.

He had settled for these, in shades of crimson and yellow. He breathed in the wonderful fragrance, imagining Jordana's pleasure in it. Next June when the old garden roses with such wonderful names as Damask, Gloire, Apothecary and Maiden's Blush were in bloom, he would walk with her in the garden, telling her of the myth and fact that surrounded each.

June, nearly a year away. Who knew where he would be in a year, or what he and Jordana would have? He wouldn't think of time. This was the day they had, and he was eager to share it with her. Plucking the single rose from its vase as he went, he crossed to the bed, kneeling beside her.

"Jordana." Her name was no more than a breath, no more than the velvet petals that caressed her cheek.

He watched as her eyes fluttered and her arms lifted, extending, stretching, reaching for him. Her lips curved in a smile, and the heavy lashes lifted over the eyes that held him captive with their secrets. Her fingers touched his face, lingering at his mouth. "Good morning." She laughed softly. "It must be morning, I feel so wonderful."

"Do you?" His voice was hoarse, unused. "Only because it's morning?"

"It's not just any morning. It's the first morning of..." As she stammered, a blush crept over her cheeks. Pink complimented by the crimson rose. "...of our time together."

"Regrets, love?"

"No regrets." The forgotten rose shattered between them, its delicate petals scattering like jewels over her breasts. "Never."

As their bodies twined, Patrick knew that whatever tomorrow brought, when there were roses he would remember Jordana as she was now.

"You did all this in just a matter of weeks?" Jordana's fingers were laced through Patrick's as they strolled through the house. Turning to the tall windows once covered with heavy drapes, she felt the light on her. "It's more than fresh paint and furniture, or even taking down Grandmother's portrait. You've swept the memories away with the darkness."

"We're beginning with a clean slate. Only good memories allowed."

"Only good," she echoed, and smiled.

"There's more."

"How could there be?" Releasing him, she spun like a child, arms outstretched to embrace all he'd shown her.

"In a day that's already perfect, how could there be more?"

"You'll see." Catching her fingers again in his, drawing her hand to his arm, he led her to the garden.

"How?" If she'd been delighted with the house, her face was a study in wonder now. She touched a fern, and then a rose, and smiled over the wonderful, silly four-o'clocks. "This garden was a wasteland only weeks ago. It had been for years. Grandmother dismissed the gardener."

"As soon as she realized how much flowers meant to you," Patrick supplied. "That's over and done with. From this day on there's no room for her ugliness and spite in this house or this garden. We won't let anything spoil Mr. Osaka's miracle. Not your grandmother, nor my mother. Only good memories, remember?"

Jordana picked a rose. It was the same as the rose whose petals were strewn over her bed, whose fragrance still lingered on her skin. Patrick had created a paradise. For a time they could remain there, untouched by the world. But the day would come when they must leave, and she wondered if moments like these would survive. Fear found a tiny foothold in a heart that wanted only to love and be loved.

The exhilaration was gone. She was so quiet that Patrick felt her fear. With a hand at her shoulder he turned her to him. There were bright tears in her eyes, weighting her lashes. "Don't. There are no guarantees in this life. So we take our blessings as they come, and we cherish them for however long we have them."

When he bent to kiss away her sadness, Jordana's arms wrapped about his neck, the rose clutched in her hand. He offered kindness and honesty, and she did not need guarantees.

* * *

The last mellow notes had barely died away when Jordana laid the guitar aside. For half an hour she'd leaned against the pillows of her bed, the instrument cradled against her body, absently drawing melodic chords from it. Her hand tarried lovingly at the strings, and even her touch drew an illusion of music from Patrick's magnificent gift.

In the quiet, Patrick looked up from his work, then laid it on his desk. She'd had something on her mind for most of the day. When he'd returned from the office, she was subdued, preoccupied. He'd bided his time, waiting until she was ready to speak. Now, as she sat Indian-fashion, her attention on her folded hands, he prodded gently. "What is it, Jordana?"

Her hands unclasped, then clasped again. "Philip called today."

"What the hell did he want?"

"It's time for the next session on the Summer Girl campaign."

"When?"

"Tomorrow, the next day at the latest."

Patrick knew now how she hated the modeling, that it had been simply to help an old friend. The dinner at Madame Zara's, the day he first saw her, had been in celebration of Philip's big break. The chance of snaring the Summer Girl project. It was to be Jordana's last assignment. "This one worries you more than the others."

Jordana nodded. She couldn't have denied it if she'd wanted to. The weekends they'd intended to share here in her house had become weeks. In those weeks Patrick had learned to read her moods. "I won't be modeling alone."

"You dread working with a stranger."

"I can't explain why."

"You don't have to."

"I know." She smiled at him. "I never have to explain to you."

"I meant you don't have to work with a stranger."

"I gave my word. I can't let Philip down."

"You won't let him down and you won't have to work with a stranger."

"How..."

"I'll work with you."

Nothing could have startled her more. "Surely you don't want to be bothered."

"It's no bother. Actually Conroy's hinted at it, and Richard Chassen helped me find you. So, you could say I owe him. Taking part in the last shots of the Summer Girl project could be considered payment of a debt."

"Surely you don't want the whole world to see us together!"

"Don't I?" He left his desk, going to sit by her on the bed. "Where is the shoot this time?"

"In the meadow where it began."

"The innocent Summer Girl has come full circle, and now she has a lover."

"Yes."

"Then I will be that lover." He kissed her lightly, not daring more, for she was far too enticing in a long tunic of yellow silk and little else. Randy had chosen well, and arranged in a prescribed order the clothing Jordana would need. She'd even anticipated that the weekend trysts would become weeks. He didn't doubt that this particular little number was meant to be an irresistible invitation. Another of Randy's little teasers. But as much as he wanted to succumb, following his own inclination to slide silk like sunlight from Jordana's body and take her to bed, there were things he must attend to first. Plans had to be made, others had to be changed if he was to make the journey to the country.

Then, he promised himself, the yellow silk would have the fate Randy intended.

"Patrick, are you sure? These pictures will be part of a newspaper campaign, as well. Even though we've hardly been out and have rarely been seen together, the last time Randy visited, she said there was gossip. For you to do something so uncharacteristic—" Jordana shrugged in dismay "—it would leave little doubt."

Patrick's gaze narrowed, and his mouth was a grim line. All thoughts of anticipated pleasures fled as he moved away from her to the window. "Are you saying you want to keep our relationship hidden?"

Jordana smoothed sun-colored silk over a bare leg. Letting her fingers slide nervously back and forth, she nodded. "I thought it might spare you some unneeded complications when..."

"I don't want to be spared. In fact, I'd like to show the world that you're mine."

Smooth silk crumpled in a tense grip. "Is that how you feel about me, Patrick?" she asked almost too quietly.

"You're mine, Jordana."

"A possession to be flaunted? Like your other women?"

"Stop." The frigid thrust of his anger was nearly palpable as he heard her uncertainty. This, more than the modeling assignment, was the source of her disquiet. "Dammit!" His resentment soared unchecked. "The other women in my life have nothing to do with us. Nothing!" In the midst of unbridled wrath he remembered the sacrifices she'd made, and knew the simple assurance that would make them bearable.

He cared for her. Dear God, he cared. He'd shown her in every other way, but a perverse fear of the power the words would give her kept them locked inside him. Just as perversely the lash of the anger he felt for his own weakness was turned on her. "If you're too ashamed to continue with me, perhaps we should end it. Go our separate ways and forget any of this ever happened."

Her face was pale, her eyes were huge and staring and God help him, even in his anger he would give all that he had, or ever hoped to have, if she could see him.

Jordana started to speak, but couldn't force the words past her dry lips. His eyes were on her, she knew it. Just as she always knew when he was near. As she knew when he was tense or relaxed, disturbed or happy. She always knew, yet today's outburst had come without warning. A conversation of a silly concern had taken a wrong turn, delving into more serious and more frightening issues.

As was his way, Patrick had cut to the heart of the matter. She had wanted to keep their alliance secret. At first it was shame, for old teachings die hard. In the end it was fear for their perfect world. Fear of the damage outside forces might inflict on it. She should have known that even in a vacuum, perfection never lasted. It couldn't. Nothing as intense as what they shared could remain static.

Touching her lips with a tongue that afforded no moisture, she asked in a voice that was only a suggestion of sound, "Is that what you want, Patrick? To have done with this? Once I asked you not to leave. Should I leave now?"

"It's your house, Jordana." Then, with unthinking cruelty, he asked, "How would you go where you can't see?"

"It doesn't matter whose house it is, and a phone call will solve the latter difficulty. Rafe and I have become good friends. He would see to my transportation." She paused, her hands painfully clasped again. "Is that what you want, Patrick? Shall I call Rafe?"

Patrick looked away. He could barely resist the need to sweep her into his lap, to hold her, giving her the simple words she needed.

And the power to hurt him as only she could.

His fists were clenched, his breath was a shuddering rasp and a muscle in his jaw flickered over teeth so cruelly gritted they threatened to splinter. With a groan, unable to hold his anger, his heavy-lidded eyes turned back to her, seeing the tumble of her golden hair framing her pale face. Feeling her trembling pulse on his lips, as surely as if they were pressed against the tender hollow of her throat. Remembering the petals of a crimson rose scattered like rubies over the graceful slope of her naked breasts. Remembering, always remembering, how beautiful she was.

His big body sagged, and his leonine head shook. The rasp in his chest became a sigh. "No," he said at last, softly. "No, Jordana, don't call Rafe. It isn't what I want."

Jordana made no reply. Her face was blank, expressionless when she nodded.

Anger was suddenly replaced by fear. Fear that he was losing her. She had slipped away from him now, concealing her feelings behind a blank expression. He couldn't bear for any part of her to be beyond his reach. There was a time when she was his without reservation. He needed to feel that now, to feel that she really was his.

"Take off your shirt, Jordana." Command ran through his voice like an iron thread through velvet.

The last bit of color drained from a face already pale, turning it ashen. Her eyes, her beautiful blind eyes, burned like crystal fire.

When she did not move, he crossed to her slowly, shedding his own shirt as he went. "Take off your shirt," he said again, even more softly to the accompaniment of the grating of the zipper of his trousers. His step was a lion's quiet pad. A predator who meant to have his prey.

Jordana was as still as carved stone, shocked by his mood. "Patrick, this isn't the time...."

"The shirt, Jordana." He stopped by the bed, looking down at her. When she still did not obey, he slipped his hand into the folds of the shirt, his hard, rough hand cupping her breast. His fingers stroked the smooth flesh and found the tender nipple. With a satyr's grim satisfaction he felt it grow rigid beneath his caress, saw her stony expression ease. The male ego was salved, and desire spiraled out of control at the sound of her quiet moan of surrender.

He forced himself to move away, letting his hands slide slowly from her body. As he watched a bright flush rise to dot her cheeks like rouge on the waxen face of a doll, an alien sensation slashed through him. Fear and shame that he did not want to recognize. His face was savage as he would not allow himself the reprieve of looking away.

Jordana listened to the roughened edge of his breathing, searching the silence for some nuance. Needing some little thing that would explain this mercurial change in him. She'd thought she knew all his moods, but she had never seen him like this before. Not even in the early days of their relationship, when he almost seemed to hate her.

This wasn't hate. It was far from hate.

"Now, Jordana."

The voice was hardly Patrick's, and she knew he was at the end of his patience. This mood that was not hate was infectious and not to be denied by either of them. Slowly her hands slid to the button at the neck of her shirt, hesitated, then clumsily moved to the next, then the next, until the last button was dispatched and the garment lay in a bright puddle about her hips. Her hand lay loosely at her bare thighs, her hair tumbled over her shoulder, brushing her breast. While excitement coursed through her like summer lightning, she craved his touch.

"Now, Patrick," she said in a voice that was strong and clear.

When he came to her, he was wondering who had been the victor and who belonged to whom.

"Patrick did what?" Dare McLachlan, a visitor to Atlanta and Patrick's friend, stared at Rafe Courtenay.

"You didn't misunderstand," Rafe assured him drolly.

"Patrick McCallum posed for a newspaper and magazine advertisement? I don't believe it."

"Believe it. The spread was in last week's *Constitution,* and should be in a future issue of some lady's magazine. They've captured the imagination of the public. They're the golden couple. Nothing about them is private or secret anymore—where they live, what they do. For love, a recluse has forsaken her seclusion." Rafe chuckled. "Patrick didn't quite expect the notoriety, but Richard Chassen, owner of the company who produces Summer Girl, is in seventh heaven. Wherever they go they're news. Our Patrick has enough of that without adding more."

"Then he's really fond of this woman?"

"Fond?" Rafe gestured to a crowd that milled about a seated woman, and to Patrick, who hovered at its fringes. Like Dare and Rafe he was dressed formally, his white ruffled shirt gleaming over the collar of a dark tuxedo. He was an impressive sight even to the two men who knew him best. Within the circle, and the object of Patrick's acute attention, Jordana sat, listening and chatting with countless admirers. Her spangled dress of pale blue and cream glittered and clung with every move as she turned from one admirer to the next.

"Good Lord! She's beautiful!" Extravagant praise from Dare, a North Carolinian who had little time for women.

"Jordana Daniel is that," Rafe concurred. "Without a doubt. But she's far more than a beautiful face to Patrick."

"From the way he's watching her, I agree. I can't say I blame him, though. When a lady that beautiful looks at another man with such interest, maybe she bears watching."

"She doesn't see that young man, Dare. Jordana's blind."

"Blind?" Dare blinked, saying the word as if he'd never heard it before. "That beautiful creature is blind?"

"Since birth." Rafe snagged a couple of drinks as a waiter passed by with a loaded tray. In the corner a hired musician began to play show tunes on a baby grand. A woman eager to dance bumped his arm, spilling whiskey over his sleeve. Rafe wondered why he bothered with cocktail parties, why either of them bothered. Even when the party was to celebrate the success of a composer-musician affiliated with one of Patrick's many subsidiaries. Regardless of the purpose of the party, neither he, nor Dare, nor Patrick or, for that matter, Jordana, was temperamentally suited to them. Given his choice, he'd conduct business in a boat with a fishing rod in his hand.

Over the sudden din Dare asked, "Did Patrick know?"

"Not at first. It isn't exactly obvious. By the time he did, it was too late."

"What happened to his last lady?"

"Maeve Delmari." Rafe supplied the name. "The usual, this time in rubies."

"She didn't seem the type to give up a good thing quite so easily."

"She hasn't. She's been lurking around. In fact, I saw her here a while ago."

"Trouble," Dare speculated.

"Maybe. But she's no match for Jordana. The beautiful lady is exactly that, a lady. Never doubt that she's as strong as she is beautiful. She'll need to be with Patrick."

"Amen."

Rafe sipped from his drink, then scowled and set it aside. "What brings you to Atlanta and this party?"

"I brought some tapes for the host to evaluate."

"Still trying to convince Jamie he should play the piano, not grow trees?"

"I'm going to work him all summer until his tongue's dragging. When I think he's ready to listen, I'll tell him what the maestro had to say."

"Dangerous work, forestry, what with all those saws and axes," Rafe observed mildly.

"Can be."

"Patrick has told me how gifted your brother Jamie is, and that he's rather unique for a child prodigy. Doesn't the boy know his hands are too valuable to risk? Lose a finger, and a brilliant career goes down the drain."

"He's young. He hasn't learned he's not invincible." Dare set his drink by Rafe's. "He doesn't stop to consider what it would mean if he lost a finger, but I do. I think of it every day he goes into the forest."

Beyond them Patrick had had enough of the syco-
phants who occupied Jordana's time. He swooped into
their midst and without apology led her away. With his
arm about her shoulders he moved through the crowd like
a battleship, discouraging any and all who would approach with a look that froze them in their tracks. When
he saw Dare, the ice melted and a smile spread over his
face.

"Dare!" He released Jordana only long enough to shake
the hand he was offered. When the proper introductions
were made and his arm was again about Jordana, he
asked, "What brings you here?"

"Jamie."

"The renegade with the magic hands." To Jordana he
explained, "Jamie is incredibly talented, but music isn't his
first love."

Wryly Dare added, "My brother would rather play Paul
Bunyan."

"How old is he now?" Jordana's voice was pitched low,
yet still it carried over the babble of the crowd.

"Eighteen," Dare drawled. "Old enough to understand what a gift he's been given rather than tossing it
carelessly away."

"A difficult age," Jordana reminded.

Dare laughed, and there was warmth and affection in the
sound. "All Jamie's ages have been difficult."

"Because of the three of them, Ross and Robert Bruce
and himself, Jamie's the most like big brother Dare. Stubborn, proud, cocky." Patrick laughed. "Shall I go on?"

"I think Miss Daniel gets the picture." In explanation
to Jordana, he said, "The North Carolina highlands are
filled with stubborn Scots. It was just our luck that two of
the worst came in the same family."

"I think you and your brother love each other a great deal, and that he wants to be like you," Jordana suggested.

"Hero worship?" Dare shook his head. "I'm no hero."

"I suspect you are to Jamie. Patrick's told me a little of your family. How close you are, what fine young men you've made of your brothers." She smiled up at Patrick. "And how often you've beaten him at the Highland Games."

A guest who had imbibed too freely at the bar lurched into Jordana, sending her stumbling against Patrick. In the second after he'd seen she was unharmed, he spun about with a look of such violence the poor man stammered an abject apology and fled.

"Careless son of a—"

Jordana's hand on his arm halted Patrick's muttered insult. "It was an accident and nothing came of it. No one was hurt beyond his pride and your temper."

"Why the hell did we come here in the first place?"

"You wanted to, Patrick."

"Well, I don't want to anymore."

Rafe looked at Dare and Dare at Rafe. They had been forgotten.

"Let's go home, Jordana, I don't like this crowd." Patrick had the grace then to remember his friends. "It was good to see you again, Dare. Jordana and I plan to get down to Carolina soon. I'd like her to meet Raven. They share a common interest in flowers." In an abrupt change of subject, "Rafe, the plane will be ready tomorrow?"

"Ready and waiting as ordered." The Creole's expression was suspiciously solemn.

"Then we'll see you at nine."

"That you will, boss." Rafe's dark, saturnine face softened. "Good night, Jordana, and good luck."

"Thank you, Rafe. Good night, Dare."

Before Dare could reply, Patrick was sweeping her from the room. Gently but firmly he brushed aside a tittering woman who wanted to make their acquaintance, and less graciously, a handsome young actor who wanted a dance with Jordana. Only the host managed a parting word.

Dare turned his astonished stare from the door. "Flowers? He wants Jordana to meet Raven because they share an interest in flowers? What does Patrick know about flowers?"

"Actually quite a lot now."

"Because of Jordana?"

"Everything is because of Jordana these days." Rafe watched the crowd, gauging how soon he could leave and how he could get past a blonde who had watched him all evening. "Tomorrow he's taking her to see a group of specialists, tops in their field. He's determined that somehow, some way, he can find a way to make her see."

"Is there any chance?"

"Not a chance in hell. Jordana's eyes were damaged beyond hope at birth."

"Then why?"

"Why is Patrick doing it? Because he can't believe anything important is impossible. We both know I wouldn't be alive today if he didn't believe so stubbornly that the impossible is possible. Why is Jordana putting herself through a grueling exercise in futility?" Rafe's voice was gruff but soft. "The lady loves him."

"So she'll go with him and hear all the heartbreaking news. I'm sure not for the first time."

"Yeah, and hurt more for Patrick when he finally admits what he wants most for her *is* impossible."

Dare shook his head. "The mighty has fallen at last."

"He hasn't admitted it yet, but he has. Completely."

"Could you choose a finer lady for him?"

"No." Rafe shook his head. "Not if I searched the world. Speaking of the world, I have a plane to see to before Patrick flies off into it."

"I have a reservation for dinner at Madame Zara's."

"Good luck." Rafe touched his forehead in a mock salute.

"To both of us. Patrick has found his."

"Yeah." Rafe stared beyond the crowded room. Night had fallen and the city was alight. No darkness in his world or Patrick's, no light in Jordana's. But times had changed in the past twenty-eight years. Medicine had changed. "Maybe tomorrow or the next day, or even the next, he'll get lucky again."

"A miracle of modern medicine?"

"Yeah," Rafe murmured. "A miracle for Patrick."

Ten

—

"That's it, Mr. McCallum. Every test, every examination concurs with all the others. Nothing has been overlooked, no mistakes made." Blunt words, delivered mercifully, without saccharine platitudes.

The doctor fell silent, and in the silence his own disappointment hovered like an echo. Papers rustled, and a chair creaked as only old leather could. Beyond the windows, massive machinery, the heartbeat of this sprawling institution, growled into the late-summer day. A fragrance drifted among harsh odors of medicines. Flowers, bright strands of hope in somber despair.

Hope. The air was heavy with it.

Some realized.

Some lost.

Patrick's chair lurched back, and his footsteps, muffled by a forest of carpet, took him to the window. Jordana knew he was standing there, staring through the glass, seeing only his own shattered hopes.

She didn't move, didn't speak. Neither of them had spoken much since the afternoon Patrick had gathered a shirt of yellow silk from a bedroom floor and thrown it away. The savage emotion of that day had never been put into words. A heartache never soothed. Its memory haunted them, changed them. What had been serene had become feverish. Their days of self-contained quiet became the seeking frenzy of social outings he insisted on but never enjoyed. They were seen and sought after, playing the role of the golden couple, until he could bear no more, gathering her up like precious baggage, rushing her home.

The hours that followed were filled with brooding and sex. Jordana no longer pretended, dressing it with pretty words. It was sex, lust, an exorcism of raw emotions that left them shaken. Dark, exciting, shattering and strangely flawed.

Now this, his quest to restore her sight. Their journey to countless medical institutions had been as turbulent as the sex. As futile. Jordana knew what the answers would be, but accepted that Patrick must hear them for himself.

"I'm sorry." The doctor spoke his regret to Patrick. He seemed to know the big Scot was as much the patient as she. "The damage is irreversible. Miss Daniel will never see."

The room was stifling. Scents borne on motionless air suddenly cloyed. Patrick drew a deep breath. In it she heard anger, despair. Denial.

"There are other doctors, other places."

"No, Mr. McCallum," the doctor interrupted, his burr more pronounced than Patrick's, but compassionate. "There are no others who will give you a different answer. Neither here in Edinburgh, nor any part of the world. There is no other answer.''

"Dammit, Brodie..."

"Accept it, learn to live with it."

"No!" Patrick was fighting the truth. Fighting hard.

"You have no choice." Dr. Brodie remained unperturbed. He had seen this before. Done it before. "Go home," he urged. "Take this beautiful lady and go. For your sake, she's trekked from country to country, hearing over and over again what she already knew. She's exhausted, both physically and emotionally. Give it up before you do harm where you mean good."

"There has to be some way."

"There is no way. For *her* sake, give it up. Go to your Highlands. Let her experience more of Scotland than the inside of hospitals. Rest. Count your blessings. In time you'll know how many there are."

Patrick turned from the window, looking to Jordana. Her face was calm but haggard. For the first time he saw how trying this had been for her. How painful to face hearing it over and over again. Yet she had.

For him.

All the angry purpose drained from him. All the strong conceit that believed he could make all things possible, that everything had its price. He'd been wrong, and in error, cruel. His own face was haggard, his shoulders bent, when with a curt nod he admitted defeat.

Crossing to Jordana, he touched her cheek, his thumb brushing the fringe of her lashes. He saw no censure, no grief, only rare courage. If he lived forever, there would never be a woman more beautiful.

The beep of Brodie's pager commanded. He was needed. His apologies were brief. What more was there to say? Then Patrick and Jordana were alone with their bitter knowledge.

"You knew." His hand still curved at her cheek, his fingers touching the fine, pale skin.

"I've known for a long time."

"Yet you subjected yourself to this for me."

Her hand covered his, holding it close. "Does it matter so much that I can't see?"

"No." The pulse at her temple fluttered beneath his fingertips. "It doesn't matter at all."

But as he went with her through somber corridors into the white light of day, he knew he lied.

Edinburgh marked another change. Their days became a sham of idyll. No matter how he pretended, Patrick was troubled, as only a strong man whose strength and judgment has failed him could be troubled. By day he played the gracious and gallant host. Teaching her of his homeland, he found a new eloquence, painting vivid pictures of the McCallum clan, its stronghold, its history, the battles fought to keep their lands. If he was eloquent by day, at night, when they were wearied by his pretense, he was a stone. Most evenings, after dinner in the massive dining room that rang hollowly of brooding restraint, Jordana found herself alone. Patrick, the soul of courtesy and convention, made polite excuses, leaving her to barricade himself behind the doors of his study.

As she'd learned more and more of his country and his people, the man she loved had become a well-mannered stranger.

"But no longer," Jordana vowed as she paced the length of a room far too familiar from other nights of pacing. Nights she spent alone, slept alone, while a polite stranger locked himself away and brooded in the darkness. They would not go on as they had. The estrangement that grew each day like an ever-widening chasm must be resolved. She wanted—no, she needed—the bold adventurer. The man who could be as arrogant as he was tender, who was as maddening as he was wonderful. Life with him had rarely been peaceful, but neither had it been lonely.

Crossing to the door of her bedchamber, she knew the risk she was taking in going to him. She could win tonight, or she could lose. But what other choice was there? Her heart was in Patrick's hands. It had been since the day he'd stepped into her life.

Squaring her shoulders, she stepped into the hall. She knew the distance to the stair and how many stone steps would take her to the lower hall. Sixty-three paces from the last step would lead her to Patrick's study.

Her footsteps beat a ghostly tattoo on ancient stone worn by the tread of the McCallums that had gone before him, by laird and family and servant. She could have summoned a servant now with a ring of a bell, but the hour was late; they would've retired. Were they not, she wouldn't have called. This was a time only for Patrick. At the massive doors she hesitated, gathering her dressing gown closer about her. Fearing he would refuse her, she entered without knocking.

The room was still, soundless. Then she heard his ragged breath, followed by the tinkle of ice against the side of a glass. "What are you doing here?" His voice was thickened by Scotch.

"We need to talk."

"Do we?" Ice tapped at the glass. "If you've come to tell me we should go home, it's already arranged. We leave tomorrow at noon."

Her hand was on the latch; now she stepped farther into the room. "I didn't come to discuss leaving."

"What did you come to discuss?" He was cold, so cold. Now that she was here, she didn't know what to say.

"Did you come to condemn me for humiliating you?" He drank again, long deep swallows. "If it gives you any satisfaction, I live with the guilt. If I should forget, there's always a yellow flower, or a scrap of yellow sky. Yellow! Everywhere I turn it's there. Then, damn my soul, I see you sliding a yellow shirt from your body."

"I'm as much to blame for that as you."

"You're innocent."

"I haven't been innocent in a long while. I could've stopped you, Patrick. With a single word. No. That's all I needed to say. We both know why I didn't."

The stillness deepened. She could imagine him standing there, drink halfway to his lips, his eyes on her, waiting.

"I wanted you then, on any terms. It didn't matter whose pride was sacrificed. Mine." She hesitated. "Yours."

"You think it was my pride.... How the hell do you figure that?"

"In my selfish desire, for want of a word then or later, you've borne a burden for an act of unbridled passion that was never yours alone."

"It was a spiteful act."

"It was a desperate act. For both of us. Each proving to the other, God knows what."

The glass was down now. She heard the soft thud of it on his desk. "I know. We both know. I seduced you, yes, but out of fear and anger. Fear that I was losing you. Anger that I cared. More than that, I needed to prove that you needed me, that you would always need me."

"I do."

He shook his great head, unsure of what he heard, wondering if she knew he had only proven how much he needed her. "You haven't blamed me? Haven't hated me?"

"If there's blame, it rests with both of us. And I could never hate you, Patrick."

He groaned, a muffled sound of relief and disbelief and something more. Something she hadn't dared let herself hope for, dared not believe. Leather crackled and wood protested beneath his weight as he sat down abruptly. Jordana waited for him to speak again. There was only his mute struggle with his thoughts, with himself. She needed to comfort him as much as she needed to love him. Going to him, her step was sure, confident, for no one would dare leave anything out of place. Not if he, or she, valued life. Patrick had been adamant in that and unforgiving. He was a hard taskmaster, but never harder than on himself.

Circling his desk, she stopped by his chair. He smelled of soap and Scotch. When she touched him, laying her hand on his shoulder, he spun to her, his arms winding about her, his forehead leaning heavily against her breasts. "I didn't know it could be like this. I didn't believe I could trust."

Trust, she had never dared hope for.

"You were a woman beyond my experience. I took, you gave. Every arrogance met kindness. Every impatience, patience. Every demand, courage and strength and, above all, grace. Anything I've asked, you've given, asking nothing in return." He drew a shuddering breath. "There was one thing I wanted to give you. I thought I could give you."

"My sight." She stroked his hair, letting crisp curls slide through her fingers onto her breast.

"I've done very little in my life that could be called kind. When I tried, I was clumsy with it, but I never meant to hurt you."

"I know. I'm sorry I can't see. I wish I could see *you*. But no matter how we wish them, some things aren't meant to be."

"And some are." He was rising, reveling in the slide of her hands down his body as he towered over her. "From the moment I saw you, no matter how I fought against it, I was destined to love you."

"Were you?" she asked softly, her face lifted to his. "Do you?"

She knew. He saw it in her radiant face, but because she needed the words she had waited so long to hear, he said them. Words he'd never said to anther woman, for there was no other woman like Jordana. "I love you."

So much that any hurt to her was a greater hurt to him, any blow to her pride was a blow to his. So much that he wanted to give her the impossible and suffered when he failed. Her sight was meant as a gift for her...not for himself. That was the pain she heard, the disappointment that even the Scotch couldn't dull.

With her hands catching in his hair, she drew him down to her. Hurts and disappointment were forgotten. His, hers, soothed by words, sweet and low, of love and honor. Tomorrow they would leave Scotland, then other truths, other realities would intrude, but they had tonight.

Jordana's fingers strayed over the strings of the guitar, with only her thoughts to guide her. Her smile was content, her music wistful. Secret doubts, the dread that threatened a life too perfect, were for the moment put away. The Daniel house was at last a house filled with love. As he did with everything, when Patrick committed himself, he did it with all his heart, without reservation. And it was she who was blessed.

In a room filled with flowers from the garden Patrick had created, she was waiting for Randy. So much had happened in the weeks since she had seen her friend and confidante. So much that was wonderful and surprising.

Seconds had crept into minutes, minutes into hours as she waited. The chime of the doorbell had her laying aside the guitar and hurrying to the door. Flinging it open, expecting to be caught in an exuberant embrace, she was met instead by a drift of heavy, exotic perfume Randy would never wear.

"I'm sorry," Jordana said, catching her breath and her poise. "I was expecting someone. May I help you?"

Silence greeted her question, but someone was there, staring at her. A woman. Frowning, her hand going to her throat to tame the sudden rush of her pulse, she asked, "Who are you?"

A rustle of clothing, the grate of a shifting shoe on the step was the only response.

"Very well." Jordana stepped back, intending to close the door between herself and the malevolence that chilled her like a wintry breath.

"No." A hand closed over Jordana's wrist. A small hand with long, brutal nails. "Not yet."

Holding herself motionless, refusing to struggle, Jordana asked, "Do I know you?"

"No, but we share, shall we say, a mutual friend."

"Patrick!"

"Ah." The voice was deep, cultured, verging on sarcasm. "You understand, then."

"What do you want?"

"To talk to you."

"We have nothing to say, Miss..."

"Delmari. Maeve Delmari."

Jordana had heard the name. The gossips at the gatherings she had attended with Patrick made sure of it. She couldn't imagine what the woman would have to say to her, but on the chance it would be to Patrick's advantage and her own to hear the woman out, she would. Pulling free of the grasp, she stepped aside. "Come in, Miss Delmari, say what you have to say. I won't offer you a seat, you won't be staying."

They'd barely stepped beyond the door when Maeve Delmari launched her verbal attack. "It won't take long, not if you love Patrick. If you don't want to destroy his life."

"I have no intention of destroying anything for him."

"You will if you persist in this arrangement."

"Our arrangement, as you call it, is none of your business."

"Oh, but it is. Because I care for him. Because I know what he needs to be happy. Because I can give him what he must have. Sons, Miss Daniel, to grow strong and tall, who will keep the lands Patrick loves. Sons who will need a mother who won't be a burden. Patrick needs a wife who walks freely beside him, not clinging to him. Who won't make him sick from being tied to her year after year. He's a virile man, a sportsman. His sons will be the same, they must have a mother who's as vigorous."

Her voice changed. Contempt became an odd mix of flattery and coercion. "Those who know him say Patrick loves you. That you're the one woman he will never leave. So you must do it. You must leave him."

"No!"

"Yes." A demanding hiss. "Leave him before what he feels for you turns to pity."

Jordana fumbled at the door, flinging it open. "Get out, Miss Delmari."

"Certainly. I said this wouldn't take long." She took a step to the door and paused. "Just one last thought. You know I'm right. You wouldn't have listened as long as you did if you didn't believe me. I only put into words what you already knew. Leave him, Miss Daniel, while the memories you take with you are still beautiful."

"Get out." Jordana was shaking. "Don't come back."

Maeve Delmari looked at her ashen face, at the slight, trembling body, and smiled. "I don't think there will be a need. Think about it. You know I'm right."

Long after the exotic perfume had faded, Jordana stood in the doorway, hearing a voice from the past calling her defective, a poor child no one could love. A woman fit for little. The tears came then, silent tears that had no end. Turning from the open doorway, stumbling, gasping for breath, she found her way to the garden.

When Randy came, she was there, hands folded in her lap, her empty eyes staring into her darkness.

"There you are." Randy rushed into the garden like a whirlwind. "Sorry I'm late. I had trouble finding the buckle you wanted for Patrick. He should look grand in it when he wears his kilt." Her tone turned to scolding as she set down a bag of wrapping paper and ribbon. "The front door was wide open. Anyone could . . ." Her voice trailed into shock as she took her first good look at Jordana. "Oh God! What's wrong?"

"Nothing's wrong." Jordana's voice was lifeless, without inflection.

Randy sat beside her, taking Jordana's cold hands in her own, seeing the tearstained face, the lost look. "Is it Patrick? What has he done?"

"Patrick's done nothing."

"Then what? You were so happy just a few hours ago. Now you look as if you've lost the most important thing in the world."

"I have."

"What happened? In just a few hours, what could have happened?"

"Later." A tear trickled down her face. She didn't bother to wipe it away, and Randy wondered if she knew it had fallen. "I'll tell you everything, but later."

Randy brushed the damp, disheveled hair from Jordana's face. "Should I leave?" The last thing she wanted was to leave Jordana as she was, but she had to ask. "Is this something you should settle alone with Patrick?"

"When he comes, I'll see him alone, but don't leave. Not until I speak with him, then I'll be going back with you."

"Going back! Why in heaven's name would you do that?"

"Please, Randy, no questions. Not now."

Randy bit her lip as tears flooded her own eyes. She had never seen Jordana like this. Not even when she'd borne the brunt of her grandmother's hate. Randy wanted to hold her and soothe her as she would Cassie, but dared not. Jordana was barely clinging to her composure. Sympathy could be her undoing. "All right. I'll make myself scarce while I wait. What should I do with the buckle with the McCallum crest?"

"Wrap it. I'd like him to have it. I'd like to think in the years to come some connection between us survives."

"Jordana, are you sure..."

"No questions. You promised." When Randy sighed and gripped her hand in acknowledgment, Jordana continued. "When Patrick returns from the office, wait for me in your car. I won't be long."

Randy didn't argue again. She was just laying the wrapped package by Jordana when she heard Patrick calling. With her head low and offering only a muttered greeting, she rushed through the house past him. She couldn't bear what was about to happen in the garden. For either of them.

"Randy!" Patrick called after her, then shrugging, he tossed aside his jacket, loosened his tie and went to find Jordana.

In the garden Jordana waited for him. Sitting as Randy had found her, as she had been since Maeve Delmari had gone. As she'd sat for hours, trying to make sense of it all. Trying to deny the truth the intruder had shown her.

How could she deny what she was?

His hands on her shoulders, his lips in her hair, had her struggling to keep back the tears she had promised herself he would not see. She knew then that all the explanations she'd planned, the efforts to make him understand, were beyond her. This could not be done with grace, but because she loved him, it must be done.

"I didn't know that days could be so long, or that I could miss you so much." The love he'd waited so long to say, was there now, in every word, every touch. He stood behind her, his hands gliding down the curve of her shoulder and back again. "I thought about finding you here, waiting for me."

"Patrick." She held herself rigid. "Don't."

"Don't?" Something in her tone warned him. He was instantly wary, aware now of the tension in her. A weight settled over his chest. "Don't what? Don't say I missed you? Don't touch you? Which is it, Jordana?"

"Neither. Both." She shook her head, not sure what she was saying. "Please, Patrick, don't make this any harder."

"Don't make what any harder?" He stepped back, his hands falling away from her.

Jordana stood, the gaily wrapped package clutched in her hand. "I have to go away."

"Go?" he asked stupidly. "Where?"

"Away from you. I've had time to think. We've known from the start we were too different. Here alone in the house today I had time to think. What we've shared has been wonderful, but it can't work."

He was reeling. He'd trusted her with his life and his heart, confident she would never hurt him. The pain now was so powerful he could only contain it with anger. "As easy as that you decide to walk out of my life?"

"It's for the best."

"Whose best?" he asked coldly. "Yours? Mine?"

"It's for both of us. Before I go..." She offered the package, holding it in the palms of both hands. After a moment she set it down on the bench. "I wanted you to have this. To remember me by."

Patrick's laugh was humorless, contemptuous. "I'll remember you, honey. I won't need any little mementos."

She heard the hurt through his anger. "I'm sorry, Patrick."

He wanted to grab her and drag her into his arms. He wanted to kiss her until she recanted all she'd said. Instead, he nodded. "Yeah, so am I."

Jordana hurried from the garden. At the gate she paused, but did not turn back. "No matter how much we wish it, some things aren't meant to be."

He heard her whisper, saw her blue dress clinging to her. Beneath the silk her breasts would be bare and only a scrap of bikini lace at her hips. In the hazy aura of the lowering sun, she was a burning flame of blue. He almost called her back, almost pleaded. Turning away, he let his eyelids close over weary, aching eyes. In their darkness a blue flame burned.

The garden was quiet. When he turned back, she was gone.

With the beat of a breaking heart, without rhyme or reason, it had ended. All that remained was a single whisper, repeated in scattered rose petals that fell like crimson tears over the grass.

...some things were never meant to be.

As twilight began to fall, he sat with the unopened package in his hand. The irony of it was not lost on him. He had given many gifts to ease his farewell. Now he had his own.

There was no ease in it.

Eleven

———

"**D**ammit, Patrick! You should be in a hospital. Anyone else who rolled a car down an embankment would be. Anyone with good sense." Rafe's argument, as others before it, fell on deaf ears.

After playing the playboy for weeks in his effort to erase Jordana's memory, Patrick had finally left the States. Rafe's hopes that Scotland would improve a Scot's mood were quickly destroyed. If anything, Patrick was more irritable, more stubborn, disappearing into his study to brood for hours on end. All culminating in an accident that should not have happened—a lethal combination of a fast car and too little sleep. Patrick never seemed to sleep anymore.

"Don't need a hospital. Liniment for bruises outside." Patrick lifted a glass of clear liquid. "This for inside."

Rafe glanced from Patrick to the magazines scattered over the massive desk. Every cover Jordana had ever done was there.

"A beautiful woman," Patrick said, following the path of Rafe's gaze. "A toast! To women." The glass crashed against the stone fireplace, and Scotch fanned into a glittering arc, falling onto the carpet like crystal rose petals. Without missing a beat, Patrick filled another glass.

As he watched him, saw the tremor in his hand, Rafe's decision was made. In unspoken agreement he'd never interfered in Patrick's life, nor Patrick in his, but for every rule there was an exception.

Jordana slept on a chaise by the pool, with Cassie playing sedately at her side. Randy set a tray of lemonade and cookies on the table, cursing Maeve Delmari roundly in her mind, as she did every time she saw Jordana's thin body and the bruised shadows beneath her eyes.

Randy had argued, long and heatedly, when she heard the story, but to no avail. Jordana stood firm. The prejudices of Emma Daniel, instilled in a vulnerable child, were resurrected in a hurting woman.

Ice shifted in the glasses, a bell-like sound against the crystal. Jordana's eyes opened slowly. For a moment she was in another time, another place, then she remembered. This was Georgia, not Scotland. Her summer idyll had ended.

"Lemonade?" she asked, hoping Randy hadn't noticed the flash of painful remembrance.

"Always, when it's hot as Hades and the calendar says October." Randy took a seat by her. "Everything reminds you of him, doesn't it?" At Jordana's nod she grimaced. "If only I'd known."

"There was nothing you could have done. Nothing I would've wanted you to do. As everything good does, it ended. If I could have foreseen the end, I wouldn't have changed a moment. For a while Patrick loved me. Remember, a lifetime can be lived in a day, or a week, or a month. I lived a lifetime with Patrick, and I wouldn't have missed it for the world."

"You were happy." Randy covered Jordana's hand.

"More than I ever dreamed to be."

"Then that's all that counts."

Unnoticed by adult minds preoccupied with other things, a sound too regular for thunder began beyond the horizon. Steadily it grew. Cassie was first to recognize its rhythm. "Mom! A helicopter!" It materialized over the tree line, coming in fast and low. "It's coming here!"

Before Randy or Jordana could react, the monstrous machine was hovering over the meadow. A slender figure bailed out before it touched down, landing in a run that took him over the meadow and the lawn.

"Rafe," Randy said for Jordana's benefit. Then, at her look of hope, she added, gently, "Only Rafe."

At the edge of the stone landing that surrounded the pool, he stopped. "Jordana."

She was on her feet. Even in a dry swimsuit and under the blazing sun, she was shivering, fearing the worst. "Patrick?" She reached out to Rafe. When he moved to take her in his arms, she clung to him. "Is he..."

If Rafe had any doubts about what he was doing, they were swept away by the anguish he saw. "There was an accident. He's alive, but he's hurting," he said gently. "He needs you."

"I thought...I was afraid..." She swayed then and only Rafe's arm kept her from falling. As he eased her down to the chaise, she struggled against him. "I have to go to him."

"Sit here while I pack a bag," Randy said calmly. "Then we'll get you dressed and you'll be ready to go." She straightened, considered a man too composed, reading the true meaning of his words. *Hurting. Not hurt.* "Ten minutes," she promised. "I suspect this emergency can wait that long." Rafe's face remained impassive. A subtle gleam in his eyes confirmed Randy's suspicion. She touched Jordana's drawn face. "Ten. Tops. And you'll be on your way to Patrick."

With a helicopter hovering on the meadow, she went to pack a bag, to send a kitten with the courage of a tiger to a lion. Randy grinned at the metaphor. Then she laughed for the first time in weeks.

Jordana frowned as she walked with Rafe. "This is wrong." The scents were familiar, not medicinal. The sounds—the tap of her footsteps on stone, the hollow hush—were unlike the hospital she expected. Then she understood. Her fingers closed over Rafe's arm in a taut grip. "This is Patrick's keep!"

"Right you are, love." With a flourish Rafe led her through the doors to Patrick's study. "Here he is, battered, too proud for his own good, but the laird himself."

"What the devil?" Patrick lurched from his chair, and the sheaf of papers he held spilled over his desk. His gaze passed blindly from Rafe to Jordana. For a heart-stopping second he thought she was a cruel trick played by a mind not quite rational. He had dreamed that one day she would stand there as she had before, with the light like sunlight on her hair and the scent of flowers drifting about her. For weeks he had dreamed it. Then he'd stopped. His nights, like his days, were bleak and sterile at last. No sunlight, no flowers.

No pain.

Gold glittered in his eyes, and the subtle fragrance of a summer garden lay gently on the breath he drew. She was no illusion. His fingers flexed, their short nails driving into his flesh. Fading bruises at his cheek and forehead were suddenly livid.

"What the hell is she doing here?" His voice was a vicious snarl. He spoke to Rafe, not Jordana, yet his stare never left her. Like a scorching flame his eyes swept over the face and body that had tormented him. She was far too thin, almost fragile. The dusting of blue beneath her lower lashes was more than the fatigue of grueling hours of travel. Her eyes glittered as with fever.

He told himself he didn't care.

Jordana fought tears of relief. Despite Rafe's assurances during their flight, she had been afraid...no, she wouldn't think of her fear. Even if he weren't a part of her life, she wouldn't even imagine a world without Patrick. "Rafe said you needed me."

"I did. Once."

But not anymore. She drooped like a flower wilting in the sun. "Patrick, I'm sorry. I thought..."

"Tell me what you thought, Jordana." There was steel in his voice, cold, cutting steel. "You didn't bother before. Tell me now. For the record, I'd like to know."

"Patrick," Rafe cautioned.

"Stay out of this, Rafe," Patrick commanded as he crossed to stand before Jordana.

"Too late. I dealt myself in days ago." Then, before Patrick could object again, he demanded, "You want it straight?" Rafe had heard the whole ugly story in flight.

It sickened him then. It sickened him now. "Ask about Maeve."

"Maeve! What has she to do with this?" Patrick's eyes flicked from Jordana to Rafe and back again.

"What indeed?" Rafe asked wryly, and because he saw that Jordana could never tell it, the story spilled out of him. When he was done, Patrick stared at him for an eternity before turning to her.

"Damn, Maeve!" Patrick exploded. There was a bitter savagery in him, but the hands at Jordana's shoulders were gentle in their urgent grasp. "Damn you for believing so little in me."

"I believed. I never stopped believing."

"And still you left me? God, Jordana! Do you think I'm a fool? If you'd loved me as you pretended, the prattling of an old woman and jealous bitch would never have driven you away."

"You're wrong, Patrick." Rafe's voice cut through his anger like a knife. "It was precisely because she loved you that their *prattling* worked. Emma's prattling years ago kept a young woman from understanding how much she had to offer the world. A young girl who became an amazing woman. Who never even considered drawing attention to herself with something as useful to herself as a Seeing Eye dog. A woman who sacrificed her own privacy to help a friend, and later sacrificed even more to the demands of a man too stubborn to admit he loved her. A woman who is a wonderful friend to one special nine-year-old, and indirectly to countless other children, but thought, because of stupid *prattling* that she couldn't do justice to being a mother. More specifically the mother of *your* children."

Rafe paused for breath as if he realized he was preaching. His gaze locked with Patrick's, and Patrick saw pain and compassion in the face some fools called cold. Patrick shook his head, clinging stubbornly to his hurt. "I'm supposed to believe the doubts ingrained years ago could touch what we had?"

"Ridiculous, isn't it?" Rafe drawled. "As ridiculous as a twelve-year-old boy, deserted by an unfaithful mother, growing into a man who was afraid to trust."

"Afraid!" Patrick turned on his friend, the hands that had gripped Jordana's shoulders drawn into tight fists.

"Yes, afraid." Rafe kept his body loose, refusing to rise to Patrick's silent threat. "There's no shame in being afraid, Patrick. The shame is in letting it rule your life."

"That's enough, Rafe." Patrick's tone was guttural.

"Is it?" Cool green eyes locked with angry, blazing blue. "Is it really?"

Patrick was first to break the stare. His eyelids drifted down over burning eyes, remembering two young children, hurt by the selfish cruelty of others. The boy became a bitter man, doubting everyone; the girl, a gentle woman, doubting only herself.

He knew now that Jordana had left him not because she didn't love him, but because she loved him too well.

Doubts, instilled by Emma and magnified by Maeve, were nurtured by his anger at his need for her, his reluctance to trust. His fall into love had been less than gracious. Taut and tight-lipped, he had left something unsaid, a need unmet. He hadn't given her the belief in herself as his only love that would have withstood all assault.

He hadn't made her know she was his life, not his burden. That without her there would be no children, no lands in Scotland, no future.

Patrick's eyes opened, meeting Rafe's without flinching. "It's enough."

He turned back to Jordana. She hadn't moved, hadn't spoken. Emotional exhaustion had her swaying on her feet like a golden candle in the wind. Yet, weary and worn, when she thought he needed her, she had come to him. Courageous and giving as always, asking nothing in return.

He had to make her see, had to make her understand how much she meant to him. That it was more than even love. "Rafe's right, I was a bitter, frightened man. Then I found a woman who was everything to me. And the man I was ceased to be. Look at me, Jordana." His hands were at her shoulders again, his grasp hard, demanding. "Look with your heart at the man you made me."

Jordana heard the edge in his voice, and remembered the fierce and gentle lover. The wounded warrior who had risked his heart at last, only to have it tossed aside.

Had she done this to him? Had she made a bitter man more bitter? She was too numb to think, too weary to understand more than that she had let the hateful prejudices of a bitter old woman and the jealous vengeance of another destroy something precious. Because she needed one last memory to take with her, she touched him, letting her hand drift over his face, over the planes and angles.

A memory.

She would never forget.

Her fingers lingered at his lips. Patrick drew a sharp breath. His hands slid slowly down her back to her hips and then away. Jordana sighed softly and, as slowly as he had, she drew away.

He had loved her. He had needed her.

But not anymore.

Stepping back a pace from his unyielding presence and clinging to the last shreds of her strength, she murmured, "I'm sorry, coming here was a mistake."

"Why did you come, Jordana?"

She shook her head. "It doesn't matter now."

"It matters. It matters a great deal."

He had moved closer, his abrupt change of mood confusing her. She didn't know what he was asking. What he wanted.

"Why, Jordana?"

She had been cold from the shock of the ordeal; now his body was like a furnace, its heat reaching out to her, seducing her. "Patrick..." She swayed toward him, her breasts brushing his chest. She shivered and began to turn away, but his arms folding about her stopped her.

"Say it." His hand stroked down the length of her hair. "Please. Say it."

For a startled instant she thought she had misunderstood, and in the next, knew she had not. Her heart faltered, then resumed a ragged rhythm, as ragged as her voice when she whispered, "I came because I love you, Patrick."

His answer was to draw her to him, holding her so tightly she could hardly breathe. "That's all that matters. All that has ever mattered."

His cheek rested against her hair, and he rocked her tightly in his embrace. The weariness of weeks melted away, and the numbness, and Jordana saw with her heart the man who loved her. "Our sons?"

"Might be daughters."

"What will I do?"

"You'll love them, and they'll love you. The rest will take care of itself," he promised.

Jordana gripped the fabric of his shirt, and her body curled into his. She had finally come home. There would be problems, but with Patrick beside her, loving her, she could do anything.

"Say you'll never leave me again, Jordana. I need to hear you say it."

"I'll never leave you, Patrick. Never."

When he bent to kiss her, she was dreaming of rowdy little boys as fiery and arrogant as their father. With a little girl, even two, to put Patrick through his paces.

Rafe left them quietly. At the open door he glanced from the McCallum buckle, in its place of honor on Patrick's desk, to the magazines with Jordana's face laughing out from them. There was a story there, of courage and love.

Patrick's voice was low. The Gaelic words, beautiful. Jordana's arms about him were silken bonds; her lips meeting his were a promise.

As Rafe turned away he was smiling.

The gentle woman, who was the sunlight she would never see, had tamed the bastard.

*   *   *   *   *

SILHOUETTE® Desire™

CELEBRATES TEN YEARS OF HAPPY MARRIAGES WITH... JUNE GROOMS

COMING NEXT MONTH

#715 THE CASE OF THE CONFIRMED BACHELOR—Diana Palmer MOST WANTED SERIES
When sexy detective—and *definitely* single man!—Nick Reed returned home, he never guessed he'd be using his sleuthing skills to clear Tabitha Harvey's name.

#716 MARRIED TO THE ENEMY—Ann Major
Embittered rancher Jonathan McBride never wanted to marry again—and certainly not to Stormy Jones, the boss's daughter. So why was he now tied to the one woman he'd vowed to avoid?

#717 ALMOST A BRIDE—Raye Morgan
Rafe Tennyson had convinced his brother to leave Kendall McCormick waiting at the altar. But when he actually met the not-so-blushing bride, he knew *his* bachelor days were numbered!

#718 NOT *HIS* WEDDING!—Suzanne Simms
Ross St. Clair had no time for any woman, but especially spoiled heiresses like Diana Winsted. *Then* they were forced together and their very lives depended on a dangerous charade....

#719 McCONNELL'S BRIDE—Naomi Horton
When Chase McConnell's wife died, he swore he'd never love again. Yet when he needed an arranged marriage to keep his daughter, he found himself falling for Prairie Skye, his "temporary" bride.

#720 BEST MAN FOR THE JOB—Dixie Browning
June's *Man of the Month* Rex Ryder and Carrie Lanier hunted through the Carolinas to stop their runaway siblings from getting married. But could the teenagers give *them* a lesson in love?

AVAILABLE NOW:

SILHOUETTE® Desire™

Something old:
Love and Marriage

Something new:
June Grooms—six sexy heroes!

Something borrowed:
Silhouette Desire, for the month of June

Something blue:
The reader who misses even one of these sensual,
sassy love stories

You are cordially invited to attend the romances of our June
Grooms—six handsome hunks who have met their matches!

JUNE GROOMS: Six sinfully sexy heroes say goodbye to their
single status—forever!

Also, watch for the Silhouette Desire 10th Anniversary Collection, with
stories by three of your favorite authors. You'll want your own
memento of this joyous occasion.

"GET AWAY FROM IT ALL" SWEEPSTAKES

HERE'S HOW THE SWEEPSTAKES WORKS

NO PURCHASE NECESSARY

To enter each drawing, complete the appropriate Official Entry Form or a 3" by 5" index card by hand-printing your name, address and phone number and the trip destination that the entry is being submitted for (i.e., Caneel Bay, Canyon Ranch or London and the English Countryside) and mailing it to: Get Away From It All Sweepstakes, P.O. Box 1397, Buffalo, New York 14269-1397.

No responsibility is assumed for lost, late or misdirected mail. Entries must be sent separately with first class postage affixed, and be received by: 4/15/92 for the Caneel Bay Vacation Drawing, 5/15/92 for the Canyon Ranch Vacation Drawing and 6/15/92 for the London and the English Countryside Vacation Drawing. Sweepstakes is open to residents of the U.S. (except Puerto Rico) and Canada, 21 years of age or older as of 5/31/92.

For complete rules send a self-addressed, stamped (WA residents need not affix return postage) envelope to: Get Away From It All Sweepstakes, P.O. Box 4892, Blair, NE 68009.

© 1992 HARLEQUIN ENTERPRISES LTD.

SWP-RLS

"GET AWAY FROM IT ALL" SWEEPSTAKES

HERE'S HOW THE SWEEPSTAKES WORKS

NO PURCHASE NECESSARY

To enter each drawing, complete the appropriate Official Entry Form or a 3" by 5" index card by hand-printing your name, address and phone number and the trip destination that the entry is being submitted for (i.e., Caneel Bay, Canyon Ranch or London and the English Countryside) and mailing it to: Get Away From It All Sweepstakes, P.O. Box 1397, Buffalo, New York 14269-1397.

No responsibility is assumed for lost, late or misdirected mail. Entries must be sent separately with first class postage affixed, and be received by: 4/15/92 for the Caneel Bay Vacation Drawing, 5/15/92 for the Canyon Ranch Vacation Drawing and 6/15/92 for the London and the English Countryside Vacation Drawing. Sweepstakes is open to residents of the U.S. (except Puerto Rico) and Canada, 21 years of age or older as of 5/31/92.

For complete rules send a self-addressed, stamped (WA residents need not affix return postage) envelope to: Get Away From It All Sweepstakes, P.O. Box 4892, Blair, NE 68009.

© 1992 HARLEQUIN ENTERPRISES LTD.

SWP-RLS

"GET AWAY FROM IT ALL"

Brand-new Subscribers-Only Sweepstakes

OFFICIAL ENTRY FORM

This entry must be received by: May 15, 1992
This month's winner will be notified by: May 31, 1992
Trip must be taken between: June 30, 1992—June 30, 1993

YES, I want to win the Canyon Ranch vacation for two. I understand the prize includes round-trip airfare and the two additional prizes revealed in the BONUS PRIZES insert.

Name _____

Address _____

City _____

State/Prov. _____ Zip/Postal Code _____

Daytime phone number _____
(Area Code)

Return entries with invoice in envelope provided. Each book in this shipment has two entry coupons — and the more coupons you enter, the better your chances of winning!
© 1992 HARLEQUIN ENTERPRISES LTD.   2M-CPN

"GET AWAY FROM IT ALL"

Brand-new Subscribers-Only Sweepstakes

OFFICIAL ENTRY FORM

This entry must be received by: May 15, 1992
This month's winner will be notified by: May 31, 1992
Trip must be taken between: June 30, 1992—June 30, 1993

YES, I want to win the Canyon Ranch vacation for two. I understand the prize includes round-trip airfare and the two additional prizes revealed in the BONUS PRIZES insert.

Name _____

Address _____

City _____

State/Prov. _____ Zip/Postal Code _____

Daytime phone number _____
(Area Code)

Return entries with invoice in envelope provided. Each book in this shipment has two entry coupons — and the more coupons you enter, the better your chances of winning!
© 1992 HARLEQUIN ENTERPRISES LTD.   2M-CPN